Creations with some Re-Creations

John Mogan

Other books by John Mogan

Max and the Smugglers
Sacha, Max, and the Animals
Teck Tales
At Nodder Butte
A Journey Towards Poetry

Order this book online at www.trafford.com
or email orders@trafford.com

Most Trafford titles are also available at major online book retailers.

Printed in the United States of America.

ISBN: 978-1-4669-8105-8 (sc)
ISBN: 978-1-4669-8106-5 (e)

Library of Congress Control Number: 2013902789

Trafford rev. 03/04/2013

www.trafford.com

North America & international
toll-free: 1 888 232 4444 (USA & Canada)
phone: 250 383 6864 • fax: 812 355 4082

To the world of fiction and imaginative literature, often more true and memorable than reality itself

Table of Contents

General Introduction to All the Stories

People love stories read aloud. Whether they're children at home, children in schools or libraries, adults at book signings or seniors in retirement homes—wherever—they all sit in silence with attention focused on a person who reads them a story. They listen to happy stories and to sad stories, to stories that rhyme and to stories that don't. They listen raptly to stories about real people, places, and times, and they listen just as raptly to stories about fantasies and unrealities.

Some experts claim a limited attention span for listeners. No. Adults and children will listen to a story from beginning to end if they understand it and if it is read expressively.

In general, stories take one of two forms. The first and most famous form is the story which starts or implies, "Once upon a time . . . ." It can deal with reality or unreality, but the secret promise is a time-line of events running from a beginning to a conclusion where everything ends happily, or (sometimes) everything ends unhappily. The second form demands a leap of imagination. It starts with the transformative question: "What if?" A change is proposed and the story moves at once toward the consequences of that change.

The stories in this collection are no exception. *Marablo* is "Once upon a time." *Moving Backward* is "What if?" The creation myth of *Wagner's Ring* is "Once upon a time", and *Sacha Artist* is "What if?" The final four, *The Stone Mason*, *The Mycenaead, Solomon Bar-Levin*, and *The Other Ring* are all "What if?" In many, the words "Once upon a time . . ." and the words "What if? . . ." are not mentioned, but one of the two openings is clear early in the story.

Marablo or The Kraken

THE KRAKEN

Below the thunders of the upper deep,
Far, far beneath, in the abysmal sea,
His ancient, dreamless, uninvaded keep,
The Kraken sleepeth: faintest sunlights flee
About his shadowy sides; above him swell
Huge sponges of millennial growth and height;
And far away, into the sickly light,
From many a wondrous grot and secret cell
Unnumbered and enormous polypi
Winnow with giant arms the slumbering green.
There hath he lain for ages, and will lie
Battening upon huge seaworms in his sleep,
Until the latter fire shall heat the deep;
Then once by men and angels to be seen,
In roaring he shall rise, and on the surface die.

Tennyson

Introduction to Marablo

The origin of this story is the poem by Tennyson quoted above. That kraken has been in existence since creation. When the world is judged by fire on the Last Day, it will rise to the surface and be witnessed by all other creatures in its self-immolation.

In this story the Kraken, after its creation, was a participant in part of the later creative processes. His last appearance in this story occurs with the gods of Greece, and then he disappears to sleep until the Final Judgment.

The Dominion Of Darkness

On the floor of the ocean dwells Marablo, the Great Kraken. There at the foundation of the world, he has lain since the separation of the land and the waters. There was a time when, far below the silver surface, his twelve tentacles stretched out like a giant black cloud to the coastlines, bays, and inlets of the seven seas. In that vast ocean, the cradle of life, he witnessed the creation of all living creatures, and watched their evolution as it unfolded. From his beginning, he learned to participate with the Maker in the awakening of consciousness in many life forms. With the Maker he shaped song in the whales, and in imitation of the Maker he shaped language in the dolphins, but he played no part in the shaping of human consciousness. That was the work of the Maker alone.

For age after age, he watched the procession of plants and animals from the sea. As each species departed for the land, Marablo grieved. His tentacles followed them through the ocean to the water's edge, but none turned back. His protectiveness went to all the creatures, plant and animal, who chose to remain in the water with him. He endured reptiles who maintained some ties with his world, and he tolerated amphibians who, in a permanent state of indecision, lived in both worlds. But from the beginning, his preference had been for the animals who could think, and his love had been for those who could talk.

Marablo guarded jealously those mammals who chose to stay with him. They were his joy. Under the Maker he had given song to the whales and speech to the dolphins. So whales he admired: profound thinkers and singers. Dolphins he loved: his laughers and jokers. They sported and frolicked unknowingly for his amusement. His vastness made movement like theirs impossible, so he rejoiced first of all in their playfulness. But in addition, they had that power he had given them which his other sea-creatures lacked—the power of speech. They could talk, and laugh like the humans who had abandoned their sea-home for the land. Marablo exulted in his talking dolphins!

Once mankind had been his most favored creatures. Not only could they talk, but like their Maker, they could create worlds. It is true that the worlds they created existed only in words, but endowed with imagination, they were closest in power to the Maker. And though their storied worlds lacked substance, those worlds were infinitely interesting to Marablo. So when the humans left the sea and crawled to dry land, he grieved for ages over their loss.

THE DIVISION OF THE EARTH

Marablo was there when the giant Titans descended from space. He watched them as they tried to dominate humans, and felt a pride in his lost creatures as they talked up to and confronted the Titans. He saw the relationship shift to become more equal when a friendly Titan stole fire from heaven and gave it to humans. They were happy times. In the clear light of those primal days, everything sparkled and shone: colors were more vivid, odors more sharp. Then the three brothers came, and everything changed.

The three new young gods pushed the Titans out into space or buried them under mountains. Then they cast lots for the world. Jupiter won the air and the heavens, Pluto won the earth with what was under it, and Neptune was left with the water-world. All of them, with shouts and laughter, rode off to survey their realms. They ignored humans, and at first were unaware of Marablo, just as the Titans had been. In sardonic amusement, Marablo watched them. Dividing up "their world" indeed!

When the young gods met again, they engaged in their first argument: who would own fire? Jupiter claimed it because he had the sun, Pluto claimed it because he had the center of the earth with the volcanoes, and Neptune put in a claim because he had (he thought) the lightning that came from the clouds with rain (water). Long arguments! The upshot was that Jupiter took lightning, while Pluto kept the volcanoes with the magma at earth center and all fires in forest or field. And Neptune? What was he left with? All cold fire: the phosphorescence in the sea, St. Elmo's fire that shines on masts and spars, and the will-o'-the-wisps of fens and swamps. But he made no fuss; he had observed that their fire destroyed what it fed on, and that his water extinguished it. "Let it be!" he murmured to himself, and they were all at peace.

"Let it be—for now!" Marablo thought.

Then the border disputes started. Jupiter had the stars, the sun and the moon, the air, and the winds, but since he owned the thunderbolts, did he own the clouds? Pluto had the vales and valleys, but did he own the standing waters that formed in them? Neptune became angry at the way his brothers tried to seize parts of his liquid kingdom. "No!" he roared. "I own all water, and that means oceans, seas, rivers and streams, as well as clouds in the sky, and standing waters that sit on the earth. They are mine!" The other two backed off and left him to manage the clouds, and the inland seas, lakes, and marshes.

Marablo, from his dwelling deep in the ocean, foresaw further difficulties at the boundaries between water and both earth and air. But again, in bitter amusement, he watched.

The Encounter

Neptune found that his bogs, marshes, brooks, ponds, lakes, seas, and ocean were enough to keep him busy. He assigned the inspection and maintenance of river, brooks, and streams to the Nereids, and kept the inland seas, lakes, and ponds for himself. His most tiring tasks were tidal waters that were at one time wet, and at another time dry, and the fens and marshes that swelled and shrank. It was a long time before he turned his attention to the vast seas themselves. And during that time, Marablo prepared himself.

They met when Neptune plunged into the ocean for a grand tour of inspection. In a deep trench, almost beyond the reach of sunlight, Neptune sensed a black presence, vast, impenetrable. As he paused to peer, a voiceless question rang in his mind, "Who are you?"

In as majestic a voice as he could manage before this massive invisibility, he replied, "I'm Neptune, God of the Waters, of the oceans and the seas, of the lakes, rivers, brooks, bogs, fens, and of all the standing waters of the world. And who are you?"

"Welcome, Great Lord! I am Marablo, The Kraken. I have been here since the water was created. Up to now, lo these many ages, I have struggled to manage the ocean and its dwellers. Lord, I welcome your arrival, your presence, and your rule, under which I am happy to continue to act—or not to act—as you desire, Great Lord!" Marablo knew that Neptune could not see who he was talking to.

"The seas," Neptune began, "appear to be in good order. I would be pleased to have you continue what you have been doing."

"Thank you, Great Lord, thank you! But I need instruction. What, Dread Lord, do you wish me to do regarding the plants and animals migrating from your kingdom of water to dry land?"

"What have you been doing about them up to now?"

"Nothing, Lord, nothing! I have lain here and observed the depletion of your kingdom."

"What do you mean by the depletion of my kingdom?"

"Great Lord, I have watched the movement of your subjects from the sea to the kingdom of your brother, the Lord of the Land, since life began. I have never seen any movement of creatures, plant or animal, from the land to the sea—but I only mention this decrease in your population for your—for your consideration, Dread Lord."

"I was unaware of that, and will need time to think on it."

"Of course! I have simply observed it. I am honored to have met you, and eager to do anything you say, Great Lord."

"Continue as you have been doing," Neptune replied haughtily, and rose to the surface of the waters to consider this meeting. At no time had he seen the entire bulk of Marablo, and he felt baffled by the encounter. He felt as if he, Neptune, had been the subject and Marablo had been the "great lord". His fingers twitched on his trident-scepter, but at that moment he had no time for problems in the ocean. He felt almost relieved to be leaving its management to Marablo, the Kraken.

And in the depths of ocean, what did Marablo think of the interview? He had observed Neptune's fingers twitching on his three-pronged fork, and saw at once that Neptune would make little or no difference to him. So he turned his mind and heart once more to the loss of his creatures to the land.

The Human Factor

The three gods were all troubled by the presence of humans. First of all, they did not want to admit the existence of any higher power which could have created thinkers and talkers. Neptune was the least disturbed, because he had met Marablo, and knew that there were other, older, higher powers. Clearly Marablo was from an age before the Titans, from the creation of the world itself. And who had done that? Neptune kept those matters to himself, and feigned puzzlement over humans with his brothers.

Then, in addition, humans possessed a gift that gave all three gods good reason to worry. As well as speech, they had the gift of telling stories, of imagining unreal things and giving them existence in words, a gift that these three gods themselves lacked. Marablo knew that deep in their hearts, Jupiter, Pluto, and Neptune wondered whether humans were to be the next race of gods, to succeed their own triumvirate now ruling the world. Marablo wondered about that himself!

Humans, unaware of the anxiety they caused the gods, digged and delved, they burrowed and burned, and did whatever they liked to the land. Pluto did not know what to do about them or about their behavior, and consequently did nothing. As a result, humans began to think that they were the lords of creation until Jupiter let fly some lightning bolts, and visited them with a few whirlwinds. What happened next was completely predictable: the humans made a god out of Jupiter, and ignored Pluto, the god whose kingdom they were despoiling. Sacrifices and prayers were addressed to Jupiter. Pluto seethed with envy, but after letting loose a few volcanic eruptions, the humans offered sacrifices and prayers to Pluto as well.

Marablo was amused at the pleasure both Pluto and Jupiter took in the mistaken adoration of humans. "What fools these immortals be!" he whispered to himself. His own attitude toward the humans changed as time passed. When they first deserted the water for the land, Marablo was hurt, but he continued to love and admire them. When the humans did anything related to the water, Marablo indulged them: when they swam, Marablo calmed water to entice them back; when they built rafts and then small boats to run over his surface, he helped them with favorable currents. When, however, humans started to fish, to kill the inhabitants of the ocean—Marablo's faithful creatures—his love and admiration turned first to dislike and then to resentment.

Marablo's feelings were mixed when he observed the continuing friendliness between dolphins and humans. At first he feared that the sea mammals might desert him and follow the humans to the land. But as ages passed, he relaxed and accepted that they would remain his creatures after all: the whales and dolphins, his joy and comfort, remained in his waters. All seemed well. He could afford to watch the perfidious humans.

So if Jupiter's winds upset boats, Marablo helped his dolphins save the humans by smoothing the waters for them. Deep in his heart he continued to distrust the friendliness between humans and dolphins, but there was no one to whom he could confide this distrust. If he told the dolphins, they might tease him by spending more time with the humans. As a result, he kept silent and watched his beloved creatures talk and sport with the disloyal humans in their wading and swimming, in their boating, and even in their fishing, when humans began to hunt his creatures of the sea as well as their own creatures of the land.

The Great Betrayal

So in the passage of time, as humans tilled the land and joined themselves into groups which they called villages and cities, Marablo watched. When they became nations and organized themselves into armies to fight over land,

Marablo listened to the tales with surprise. When they took to shipbuilding and learned to row and then to sail over the surface of the ocean, Marablo admired. When they had sea battles and killed each other, Marablo was amazed. But wars ended and they returned to fishing. Marablo knew that sometime he would have to act against them, but not yet!

A happy age passed. Humans living by the sea built boats that were bigger, boats that were better, and then boats that harnessed the winds of the air. They called and played and sang with the dolphins. Marablo rejoiced.

Neptune, excited and pleased by the humans and dolphins, appeared often, driving his seachariot and blowing his great conch horn. Marablo envied Neptune his shining appearance, but despised his conceited antics on the ocean. Humans thought of Neptune as a god, worshipped and prayed to him for safety and success on the water, and then for help in fishing. Dolphins swam with the ships, leading them to schools of fish, and later driving schools of fish to the fishing fleets. Marablo waited to see what Neptune would do.

Neptune preened, posed, and did nothing. He granted their prayers for success in fishing. Marablo trembled in anger and astonishment, and the oceans shook. But he settled back in watchful resentment.

Then the humans killed a whale. Marablo's response was reflex: he overturned their ship and would have killed them, but his dolphins, shouting and chattering, scooped up the crew and carried them to the land.

Marablo gathered part of himself around Neptune and halted him as he rode in his chariot. Neptune, trapped in an inky ocean, had to listen.

"Dread Lord," Marablo began, "O God of the waters, of the oceans and the seas, of the lakes, rivers, brooks, bogs and fens, and of all the standing waters of the world, give me, I pray you, guidance at this time."

"With what do you need guidance?" Neptune asked standing up helplessly on his sea-chariot, his seahorses immobilized.

"Humans have for many years been killing your fish-subjects . . ."

"Yes," Neptune interrupted, "I gave them permission. They prayed to me, and offered me sacrifice; so I granted the boon of fishing, and asked the dolphins to guard and guide them."

There was a pause. Marablo was too astonished at what he had heard. Did this god believe that he controlled or ruled the dolphins—his, Marablo's, dolphins? He trembled with rage, and Neptune's chariot shook.

"Ah, Dread Lord, then it was you who gave them permission and leave to kill your subjects. But now they have killed one of their own; they have killed a whale, a thinking mammal like themselves, a creature . . ."

"Yes," Neptune interrupted once more, "I told them that they could kill the big fish also."

Marablo was stunned. Did this deity believe that whales were fish? In the face of such colossal ignorance, he saw the futility of continuing. "I see," he whispered and melted away, knowing that he would get no support or help from this vain god. His black shape sank into darkness. Neptune sensed his departure and was puzzled for a moment, but he shrugged, and continued the interrupted ride in his sea-chariot.

The Conclave Of Dolphins

In the ocean depths, Marablo brooded for seven years. Then through his gigantic body, through every tentacle, into every bay and river, he sent a summons to his dolphins, "Come to me, my dolphins, come to me!"

By the hundreds and thousands they came, gamboling and leaping, gray shapes against the glinting water. In an athletic and gymnastic display never before seen from the beginning of the world, they came in schools and families, shouting and laughing to sport above Marablo. Silver on blue, they shimmered above his great spreading blackness, spelled out his name,

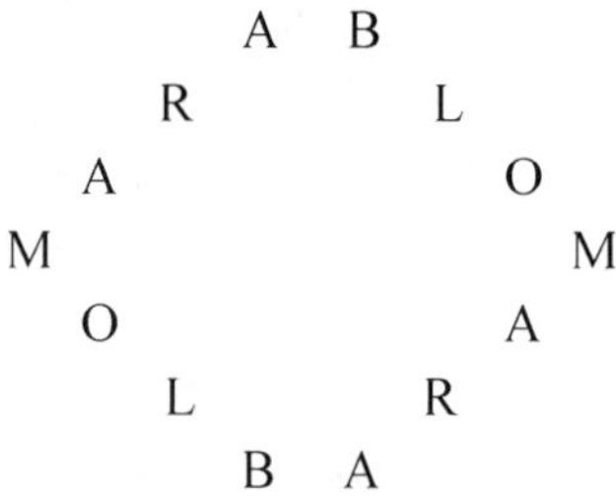

and shouted it three times all together, before they settled into quiet circles swimming over him.

"Welcome, O Dolphins of the world, welcome you living images of the joy your creator took in his own creation, welcome! I wish to hear your experiences and your thoughts regarding the humans who left you and the sea long eons ago, and moved ashore. Speak!"

Praise and satisfaction poured out at that command. They chattered and laughed about the happy bond between themselves and the people of the land. When it had died down after two days, Marablo continued, "Like you, I admired and loved them. We know that they've killed many of our fish in the sea, but they've also killed many of their own animals ashore, and we've seen them kill each other: that is their nature."

Choruses of agreement filled the air. They churned about in excitement affirming what Marablo had said. Once more, as it died down, Marablo continued, "But now there is a great change. They have murdered one of your cousins, a whale! What do you think of that? Speak!"

The dolphins swam about. From the question they knew that great Marablo was angry. They had not thought in terms of *murder*. The oldest one asked, "What would you like us to do about the death of our cousin?"

"I don't know," Marablo sighed. "I grieve for the loss, and I miss the voice and the song of my whale. I've seen the humans kill each other, and kill other animals of the land. That's not my concern. But I grieve that humans, who left us so long ago, would steal away our fish and now turn on one of your own, a fellow-mammal, and kill here in the ocean."

A low murmur of agreement came from the dolphins. "We did not think in terms of murder," many of them murmured. "We thought only about helping our human friends." And so it went from all of them.

When they fell silent, Marablo continued, "I can understand your involvement. You are friendly and helpful. That is your nature, which I love and admire. But the humans! They plan hunts. They kill each other! Now they are killing our own! What is to be done?"

"We can warn the whales. We can distract the humans. We can divert the ships." As suggestions flowed on, hope rose in Marablo.

When they all had finished, Marablo began, "Continue to help them, play with them, save them! Follow all your own suggestions: warn the whales, distract the humans, divert the ships. But—but, if they kill a whale, and their ship founders, do not save them."

"O Marablo!" many shouted, "Do you think we can change our natures to do that last thing you ask?"

"Hear me! Listen to me!" Marablo pleaded. "Only in this one trivial circumstance do I seek your help. If they kill a whale and their ship founders, do not save them. It is not much I ask. Indeed, it may never happen!"

"Marablo! Marablo! Can we let humans, our fellow beings who can talk, die in the sea?"

"Hear me again!" cried great Marablo. "Listen once more to what I ask. If your plans of distraction and diversion work, you may never need to do anything. I am making only one request: if they outwit you and kill a whale, leave them. That is all."

"But why must we do what you ask. It betrays our human friends."

"But the whales are your fellow-beings who can think, and sing. They remained with you here. Humans started in the sea, but they chose to leave the sea, to leave us, for the dry land. Now they return to kill some of our own. My request is limited: only if they kill a whale and their ship sinks, only then do I ask you to withhold help. Maybe they can survive in the sea from which they came. It is a test, but I make this simple request of you. That is all."

"We shall cooperate," the dolphins promised reluctantly, for they knew that the humans would not survive the test; they would drown.

"Thank you," Marablo sighed, and was gone. Shrieking and shouting, the dolphins dispersed in blue and silver curves.

The Desecration

Years passed. Marablo brooded and watched. Neptune rode about looking less and less like a God of the Waters, and more and more like a human. His conch-horn blew constantly. From shore to shore he traveled, listening to prayers, accepting sacrifices, and ignoring Marablo.

In the depths, Marablo lay, every fiber of every tentacle alert to the movements of his fish, his whales, and his dolphins. All too well he knew that this watchful peace would end. Much joy had left his life. The songs of whales thrilled him less; the laughter and chatter of dolphins amused him less, and the antics of humans in ships no longer filled him with surprise.

Human boldness, under the favor and protection of this upstart god, rankled and hurt. He watched the first fishing fleet with annoyance. He saw the ingenuity of seining nets, of crab-traps and lobster pots, and kept silent as Neptune offered the fish, his subjects, to ingratiate himself with creatures from his brother's kingdom, humans who had deserted the watery realm. And why did Neptune squander his fish, his subjects? Because the humans worshipped him! Because the humans sacrificed to him!

At moments, Marablo had been tempted to upbraid the dolphins as a group for being involved in the worship of this new god, but he knew his dolphins well. They saw both through and past the god. Then Marablo recognized with a stab of jealousy, that his dolphins wished to spend more time with humans.

Finally what he and his dolphins had tried to avert for those years happened. A ship sighted, followed, and killed a whale! Marablo saw the new weapon—a harpoon—and felt the attack almost as a stab to himself. He pulled the ship into the depths and drowned all the fishermen. Whale and fishermen died together.

Within a day, a school of dolphins requested an interview, and Marablo hung in black majesty under them.

They began, "A whale has been killed."

He replied, "A whale has been murdered."

They responded accusingly, "A fishing ship sank and you murdered the crew."

He responded, "I sank the ship and the crew drowned."

"We carried the bodies back to their families, and Neptune officiated at their funerals."

Marablo trembled in amazement and anger. Then he began, "Did you say that you carried the bodies back to the families?"

"We did, and we attended their funerals on the beach where the bodies were burned." The dolphins swam about in gray swirls, but as the silence stretched, they flipped in agitation.

Then Marablo spoke, "And what recognition did you—or Neptune—give to the whale they had murdered?"

"We did nothing."

"What did he do?"

"Nothing."

Once more, the dolphins swam restlessly about individually, in no formation, thinking of their failure to acknowledge the death of their cousin.

"So we come," began Marablo, "finally to the question of loyalty. To whom do you give primary allegiance?"

The dolphins looked at each other, but there was no sound except the gurgle of water. Then an ancient matriarch began, "Marablo, years ago we promised to refrain from aiding humans in their efforts to hunt whales. We have done that. We have warned whales and diverted ships. We have shown our loyalty. But Marablo," she went on, "we cannot swim about doing nothing as humans drown. We laugh together, we talk together, we play together. We cannot let them drown, even if they murder our cousins."

"Why," Marablo asked, "do you feel you owe this protectiveness to humans more than to your whales?"

"Marablo, we talk and discuss, we play and joke, we do all these things with humans, and with no other creature. We are like them, and they are like us. We can speak, we can talk together . . ."

"Enough! Leave me. I must think—I must think before I act."

The dolphins dispersed, and Marablo sank into the depths. He could see clearly where the incredible destructiveness of humans would lead—to the wasting of the land, to the pollution of the air, and to the emptying of the sea. Over all of this he brooded.

The Sad Solution

Marablo lay at the foundation of the world in despair. He could not face the course of action toward which he was being inexorably led. He grieved, and procrastinated.

Then another whale was harpooned. Marablo seized the ship by a tentacle, and in full view of his dolphins, he shook the fishermen into the sea, and smashed the ship down onto their struggling bodies. The dolphins keened, and swam away in sad arcing curves. Marablo withdrew into his black trench and waited for the silly god of the oceans, ponds, and standing waters.

The following day, in a blare of conch-horns, Neptune rode to the black trench and shouted in an angry voice, "You destroyed one of my ships and killed my fishermen without asking for my leave or permission. Explain your behavior to me, and perhaps now we can settle your role under my rule."

There was a silence. Then Marablo started, "Dread Lord, they are not *your* fishermen or *your* ships. They are the subjects of your brother, Pluto, and they murdered one of your true subject, a singing whale. They may not do that."

"If I say . . ." Neptune began, but a black body bore him through the waters to the surface, and a tentacle, giant and black, lifted his chariot high into the air, and set it down on a small islet, slowly, contemptuously. "Do not speak to me like that, Dread Lord," Marablo roared. "I do not choose to fill any role under your—your rule. The time has clearly come for you to manage *your* fishermen and *your* ships on *your* ocean. I will no longer continue to do the work I have done since Creation. The governance of all the world of waters is now entirely in your hands."

In a silence that followed, Neptune trembled under that unassailable power. Then Marablo continued, "What I do now, I do in grief and sadness. You will not see me again, so don't seek me! I repeat, don't seek me!"

Neptune fled as Marablo sank to a bottom below ocean-bottom. There, at the center of creation, Marablo undid a part of the creative act in which he had participated: he removed the dolphins' ability to speak. No longer could they talk with humans.

And no longer had Marablo any joy. He withdrew his twelve tentacles from the shores of the coastlines, bays and inlets of the seven seas. He folded himself into his great black trench, and over an age and ages, he willed himself to sleep.

THE KRAKEN

Below the thunders of the upper deep,
Far, far beneath, in the abysmal sea,
His ancient, dreamless, uninvaded keep,
The Kraken sleepeth; faintest sunlights flee
About his shadowy sides; above him swell
Huge sponges of millenial growth and height;
And far away, into the sickly light,
From many a wondrous grot and secret cell
Unnumbered and enormous polypi
Winnow with giant arms the slumbering green.
There hath he lain for ages, and will lie
Battening upon huge seaworms in his sleep,
Until the latter fire shall heat the deep;
Then once by men and angels to be seen,
In roaring he shall rise, and on the surface die.

Tennyson

THE END

Moving Backward

INTRODUCTION

Moving Backward is a short piece on political "spin" and an impossible consequence presented as a reality. The true purpose of a change affecting the environment is dressed up in words like "improvement" on what previously existed. The Handbook quoted dates from the 1990's. I cannot vouch that it remains as I quote it.

I

In 1963, NASA acquired the northern half of Merritt Island on the east coast of Florida to build a Space Station. For centuries birds had stopped at Merritt Island in their migrations north and south. To accommodate the birds,

NASA left the northern quarter of the island with its miles of beaches, its marshes, and its pools as a bird sanctuary, and built the new Space Station on the widest part of the island south of that sanctuary. They separated the two areas with a chain-link fence. Then they constructed several milieus and environments to suit all species of birds.

NASA hoped that the constructed milieus would continue to attract the birds in their migratory flights, but would keep them away from the Space Station. That sounded like a noble aim, and for many people the bird sanctuary was a brilliant product. But almost every time humans try to improve on or modify nature, there is some unforeseen result, sometimes good, and sometimes bad.

There is a handbook written about the sanctuary called *Black Point Wildlife Drive*. Some of the wording bears examination and explanation. From page 4:

> *p.4 When NASA acquired the land that is now the refuge, local cities began to grow and an effective mosquito control program was <u>needed</u>. <u>Water control structures</u> were installed to manage water levels and control mosquito populations, while also creating important habitat for migratory birds. In some areas, the marsh was restored to its natural state for fisheries management. <u>The refuge feels</u> all habitat types are important and strives to provide habitat for a variety of wildlife.*

There are three phrases underlined that require explanation. The handbook states that "an effective mosquito control program was <u>needed</u>." The question about the word "needed" is simply, "needed for whom?" It is clear that it is not for the mosquitoes, though the handbook claims in the last sentence that all habitat types are important, and that the refuge strives to provide habitat for a variety of wildlife (except, of course, mosquitoes).

"Water-control structures" are explained later. They are pipes located in dikes that separate the impoundment from the lagoon; then boards can be installed on the ends of the pipes to hold more water in the impoundment, or can be removed to drain it. "Pipes and boards" does not have the authoritative and professional ring heard in "water-control structures?"

When the handbook claims that "The refuge feels that all habitat types are important," it is the managers of the refuge that have a feeling about all habitat types (except mosquitoes). The refuge itself cannot "feel" anything.

On page 5 of the handbook, there is this passage:

> *p.5 While nature has provided a blueprint that is difficult to improve upon, the refuge can manage its lands and waters in ways that <u>benefit</u> wildlife. This may include regulating water levels to meet the needs of different fish and birds. Or it could mean using <u>prescribed fire</u> to open up areas of dense vegetation for feeding and nesting habitat. Using many management techniques to preserve, improve, and create wildlife diversity is one of the most important tools to <u>managing wildlife</u>.*

Again, questions arise about how the underlined word "benefit" is to be assessed. Whose benefit is being spoken of? "Prescribed fire" is defined later as "controlled burning." Finally, can wildlife be "wild" if it is "managed?" It sounds like an oxymoron—a self-contradiction. On page 12 this appears:

> *p.12 Through conservation and careful management, the refuge has remained a good place for wildlife to*

> *live. Whether through controlled burning, water control structures, or merely planting native species, **we** seek to insure quality habitat will always be available for wildlife and for you and future generations of Americans to enjoy.*

All the statements and claims are from a human point of view as if humans can really understand how birds live in an unnatural habitat.

II

When scientists claim that evolution is the survival of the fittest, they mean that in the crucible of the natural world, those living organisms that can adapt will survive, and those that cannot adapt will die or, as species, will become extinct. The context for the entire process is an adverse environment. When there is no adversity, then all organisms will simply live and survive.

In truth, the wildlife sanctuary seeks an environment comfortable enough to keep all the birds north of the chain-link fence.

> *Salt marsh habitat is ideal for hiding. There will be found egrets, herons, and American alligators. Wetlands provide many benefits with little cost to us. Wetlands control flooding by storing excess water, and act as filters for silt and chemicals, thereby reducing pollution in our water supply.*

The human viewpoint in the handbook—as in "our water supply"—is so taken for granted that readers accept it without a thought. From a mosquito's viewpoint, it reads very differently. And from a bird's viewpoint, it reads differently also. The truth is that managers have manipulated both environment and wildlife to purposes that they consider necessary for the space station, but they present what has been done as more beneficial to humans and to wildlife. Since the birds arrive and depart each year, the habitat must be managed so that the birds make as little impact as possible on the station and the humans who live near it.

The Merritt Island National Wildlife Refuge is not natural. Humans have made a series of artificial habitats that remove any remote resemblance to the adversity that can occur in nature's crucible. Without the impetus to evolve, there are some creatures that will remain as they are (armadillos and alligators for example); then there are some that will continue the migrations as if there were no change on Merritt Island at all. But there may be some that, in a comfortable habitat, would remain year round. A different question then arises: what if, instead of remaining stable in their present form, a species began devolving or changing back toward the ancestor from which they evolved to the present form.

III

What if in the heart of the wildlife refuge, inside the twelve artificial environments created by the wildlife refuge managers, a flock of ducks remained year round in one of the habitats comfortable for them. Since they did not have to fly or work, they began to increase in size to become, in the 1990's (over a period of thirty years), a former species, the Giant Duck (*quackus giganticus*), 5 feet long, and 2 feet high, with webbed feet 1 foot across.

The footprints they made as they moved about baffled the managers of the refuge where there were no records of such creatures. Employees at the refuge may not carry guns, so unarmed workers had to search for the birds making those tracks. The search was desultory and quickly abandoned.

In subsequent clutches of eggs from the giant ducks, the ducklings began to lose their feathers, and were born with bare skin as though already plucked. The next clutches slowly reverted to ducklings born with scales instead of feathers. They had devolved to a primitive dinosaur-form of ducks, the quackosaurus.

With subsequent hatchings, broods were born with leathery scales, incapable of flight, and carnivorous. This was the dread *quackosaurus cannibalis*, pattering about on giant webbed feet, and consuming any creature that crossed its path.

Visitors over the years had reported hearing bird sounds that they could not identify. Most ornithologists claim that a duck sounds like an oboe. As the devolution went on, some visitors reported a sound more like a *cor anglais* or a tenor oboe. In 2005, as the devolution went on and the duck increased in size, visitors heard a lower sound, more like a bassoon. And with the ducks' size, the bassoon sounds shattered the windows of pickup trucks and SUVs.

As the carnivorous form destroyed more and more birds and animals, a posse of hunters organized by the refuge, began to hunt for the bird-killer loose in the sanctuary. Their amazement was as great as the family of giant ducks they finally cornered, standing protectively over a heap of bones and rotting meat.

Did the managers recognize a bird form that humans had engineered by forming perfect habitats—habitats that offered no chance for the creatures living in them to evolve? Their answer was "No." They had no idea of their responsibility for that devolution.

And what does all of that say to human planning for the prosperity of wildlife and the effects of that prosperity on any natural life form? It may continue as it is (we hope). But it may devolve, like the duck, from bird back to dinosaur.

Imagine a quackosaurus next to the Space Station in Florida!

So in engineering wildlife refuges for birds, humans could, in their unintentional way, arrest survival of the fittest and start devolution. Such a process, devolution, creates a problem for the Creationists and advocates of Intelligent Design. That dinosaur-duck mentioned above stands as living proof that while Creation and Intelligent Design might indeed exist, there has to be room for evolution and with careful human management, as the quackosaurus proved, for devolution as well.

The End

Wagner's Ring Cycle as Creation Myth

INTRODUCUTION TO WAGNER'S RING OF THE NIEBELUNGEN

Wagner's opera cycle starts with the RhineMaidens, the RhineGold, and its theft by Alberich, Lord of the Niebelungen, the race of dwarfs under the earth.

This story presents one cycle of creation on the earth. It starts when the entire planet was water with no land, and shows the passage through a race of beings—gods, humans, giants, and dwarfs—in a fight for power, and a return of the entire world back to water.

In this Re-Creation myth, as in all Creation Myths, many "Why?" questions are unanswered and unanswerable. These things just happen.

Creation and the Gathering of the Gold

Once there was only water. The world was one wide ocean. Winds drove the waves about until storm-clouds and sea-spray hung everywhere. In the sunlight, the globe glistened like a silver ball. As it turned, the pull of the sun and the power of the winds drove tides higher and higher until part of the planet broke off and flew into an orbit around it. That part became the moon, with the same face turned forever toward its original home, the world of water.

The sun and the moon then shared control of the tides; so the waves, whipped by the winds, followed now the sun, and now the moon. As time passed, the sun and moon gradually approached each other in the heavens until the moon passed in front of the sun, eclipsing it. In the darkness, their combined pull on the tides drew all the waters of the world to one side where they climbed toward the powers that drew them. On the other side of the earth, away from sun and moon, land was born as one great continent.

The new land divided the seas. The planet shook, volcanoes erupted, and mountains rose. Where everything had been silver before, now color stained everything. The dust rising from the dry land, with the smoke and dust pouring from the volcanoes, lay suspended in the air and the sky blazed in sunrises and sunsets. The dust painted the sky and the world glowed with color.

The power of the winds over the waves fell, the waters ebbed, and the sky was washed clean of clouds and spray. Erda, Living Power of the Earth, awoke and created order above the earth, on the earth and beneath the earth.

Under sun and moon, the whole world shone as blue ocean, brown land, and prismatic color in slanted light. Clouds formed and rain fell. From the highest mountain, a great river formed and flowed to the sea—the Rhine.

From Erda three water-creatures emanated—the RhineMaidens. Over eons they gathered into one place in the river all that was bright and shining, gold dust and gold nuggets, a hoard that developed powers which only the RhineMaidens could understand.

The Occupation Of The World

Ages passed. Onto the surface of the earth, Midgard, crept many creatures bred in the oceans—plants and trees, animals and birds. Among those creatures were two thinking races: slow-plodding giants and quick-moving humans.

Beneath the earth, through caves in Nibelheim, crept the dwarfs, a race of people bred by the earth itself. They were the Nibelungen, crafters in metal and stone. Their blacksmith was Mime, and their leader was Mime's brother, Alberich.

Where Erda lay in the earth, a giant ash tree grew, binding sky, earth, and underworld together. The roots of Yggdrasil spread in Nibelheim, its trunk passed through

Midgard, and its leaves and branches stretched through the sky.

For ages upon ages, life evolved slowly. Then, into the sky from the depths of space came the gods, the Aesir. Votan was their king, and Frikka, his mate. Their kin were Thor god of thunder, Freya, goddess of youth, and Logi, the sly god of fire, along with many others. They renamed the sky "Asgard"—the god-world.

For many more ages, creatures in all three worlds prospered and multiplied while the RhineMaidens guarded their gold and sang its praises endlessly.

Votan, the king of the Aesir, was the first ceature to look beyond his own kingdom and covet power and dominion over all the earth. He felt vulnerable in the airy spaces of the sky, where he and his folk blew with the winds around the world, dwelling in pavilions of flying cloud.

He and Frikka attached a cloud-tent to Yggdrasil, the giant ash which stretched through the three kingdoms. From Erda who dwelt in the earth by that ash tree, Votan learned that the water flowing at the foot of the tree came from the Well of Wisdom, but to become wise and to see beyond appearances, one had to sacrifice an eye. Votan immediately plucked out one eye and drank the water.

He learned many things. If he carved all his oaths and contracts in runes on a spear cut from Yggdrasil, the giant Ash Tree of the World, all creation would hold them immutable. And he learned that if he tamed the two great Ravens perched in the Tree, they would serve him. He tamed them, Thought and Memory, to perch on his shoulders. Each day they flew over the world and reported all that they saw and heard.

In time, Votan and Frikka grew tired of their tent-home. They called all the gods to a Council—a spectacular gathering with lightning, columns of cloud, and the ghostly fire of Logi flickering everywhere.

Their voices rang like thunder, and they made a great covenant: all the gods vowed allegiance to Votan if he would guarantee a permanent home to end their ceaseless drift on the winds about the world. Many days and weeks passed in discussing how to do it.

At the end, Votan gave his oath to accomplish two goals, carved in runes upon his spear, witnessed by his ravens Thought and Memory, and by all the gods:

First of all, he vowed to build Valhalla, a fortress of ice and cloud in Asgard, among the branches of Yggdrasil, where they might dwell together forever.

Secondly, he vowed that his nine daughters, the Valkyries, would search the earth and canvass the souls of the bravest warriors that died in battle to form an army for the defense of Valhalla and the conquest of all Creation.

He proposed a third goal: to contract out the building of Valhalla to the Giants of Midgard, to be paid for, he suggested softly and hesitantly, with Freya, the blond goddess of youth and beauty.

Protests to that proposal rang from every side. Frikka warned that the gods would age and die if they lost Freya; nearly all the others shouted “No!”, refusing to give her up. Three gods were silent: Votan because he could think of no other payment that the giants would accept, Thor because he trusted Votan, and Logi because, in slyness, he was already devising an alternative plan.

With a shower of sparks Logi leaped up, commanding silence and attention by his dancing fires.

“Are you all mad?” he asked. “Do you not understand that Freya is only to be offered like bait so that the giants will accept the offer while we find alternative means of payment?" Many of the gods began to nod wisely (except Freya). Votan felt uneasy about Logi's intervention, but was relieved that all opposition to his plan disappeared.

Some of the gods pointed out that if the contract with the giants were written in runes on Votan's spear, it would be unchangeable. But Votan raised his spear on high, with a final word, "Nevertheless . . . ." They dispersed in silence.

Logi smiled slyly across at Votan, but stayed above in Asgard; Freya joined Thor and Votan for the descent to Midgard, where they hoped to hire Fasolt and Fafnir, the mightiest of the giants, to build their fortress.

The giants gladly agreed to build whatever the gods wanted in exchange for Freya, goddess of youth and beauty. Votan was uneasy, but glancing up at the sky he saw Logi's restless fire-trail. Counting on Logi as he never could in the past, he slowly and carefully carved the contract with the giants into his spear. The construction of Valhalla began.

THE FIRST THEFT OF THE RHINEGOLD

In the same way that Votan had come down from Asgard to Midgard, from heaven to earth, so Alberich had come up from Nibelheim to Midgard, searching for treasures on earth-surface. What a change for him from the eternal stillness of the deep caverns, or the deafening stifling smithies in the mines to the fresh greenness and perfumes of Midgard. Stars shone and clouds crossed in ever-changing patterns against a pale sky while color was everyrwhere. Alberich loved and hated what he experienced. But his eyes were drawn to a light that shone in the sky above the river Rhine. He recognized the aura of gold. By night he crossed plain and hill, guided by the shining RhineGold.

Alberich was ugly, stunted, and mean. He was astonished at the Rhine where the beautiful RhineMaidens swam around praising their gold. He tried first to bargain with them, then to seduce them, and finally to bully them. They laughed at him, and mocked him with the wonders of the hoard.

They said that the RhineGold was beyond price, and chattered on explaining why. A helmet made from the Gold would allow the wearer to assume any shape or form—even invisibility. A Tarnhelm! A Ring forged from the Gold could give its wearer power over his fellows, over Asgard, Midgard, and Nibelheim, and if the wearer had the skill, over all of the planet, lands and oceans, and even over the universe. Perhaps they talked too much of the gold's strange powers, but they felt safe revealing all they knew about the RhineGold for a good reason: only a person who renounced all love could hold the hoard of Gold, and they were certain that Alberich could never do that.

But watching them swim around, listening to them mock him, and feeling the pull of the RhineGold, Alberich changed. In rage, he renounced all love, and seized the gold. With all of it on his back, he scuttled away toward a cave leading to Nibelheim, while the RhineMaidens, weeping and wailing, waved their arms about crying piteously, "Give back the Gold! Give back the Gold!"

The only living creature who observed the seizing of the RhineGold was Logi, who had always been curious about the hoard and its powers. Muffling up his sparkling cloak, Logi followed Alberich down the cave to Nibelheim, and watched. Alberich first fashioned a Ring with which he enslaved all the dwarfs, driving them to a ceaseless search for gems and precious metal. Then Alberich summoned his brother Mime, the smith, to forge a helmet. That was enough for Logi, who had overheard what the RhineMaidens claimed. He drifted back up through the cave to Midgard, and on up to Asgard.

While the giant Fafnir was putting the final touches on the shining castle, his brother Fasolt came to claim Freya from Votan. Trapped into his bargain, Votan released Freya to Fasolt, and at once the gods began to fade and grow old. Votan quickly called back Fasolt to say that he would offer a better bargain the next day. Fasolt nodded in agreement, but insisted on holding Freya down in Midgard until the morrow.

The ravens Thought and Memory were silent; Frikka was not. She chided and upbraided Votan for his covetousness in wanting a fortress, and for his folly in using Freya as payment. In desperation Votan called on the god he trusted least, but the one whose craft and guile might find a way out of his contract with the giants. He called for Logi, the god of Fire. "Logi! Logi! Logi!"

In flickering flames, Logi appeared. He listened, wide-eyed, as if he had never heard the problem before. He told Votan and Thor about Nibelheim, about Alberich, about the RhineGold, the Tarnhelm, and the Ring. Could they be the alternative payment? Votan wanted the Ring, Thor wanted the Tarnhelm, and the giants could have the rest of the RhineGold. Logi said he wanted nothing for himself. Votan listened unbelieving. But a problem remained: how to get the gold? Logi offered to lead them to Alberich if they would let him, Logi, do the bargaining. When Votan and Thor agreed, Logi led them down from the clear skies of Asgard through the perfumed airs of Midgard to the fiery caves of Nibelheim, the underground kingdom of the dwarfs.

The caves were dim with smoke from the forges. Hammers rang like thunder. Crowds of dwarfs swept past gibbering with fright before Alberich, wielding a whip and wearing the Ring.

When he saw the three strangers in his kingdom, Alberich stopped.

"Who are you, and what are you doing here?" he demanded.

Cringing slightly, Logi spoke, eyes downcast, "High in Asgard we heard of your power, and have come to admire you."

"But what do you want?" Alberich peristed.

"To admire, only to admire!"

Alberich turned from them and screamed, "Mime! Mime!"

Fawning, with eyes darting about, Alberich's brother scuttled in holding a metal visor, "Here it is—here it is—I just finished!" He sank to the floor holding up the helmet. Alberich seized it and kicked Mime, who shrieked and crawled away.

Glaring at the three gods, Alberich placed the helmet on his head and became a giant fire-breathing dragon. Votan and Thor blanched behind their calm exterior; Logi feigned a condescending amusement.

"Bravo! Bravo! Very interesting!" He smiled and turned away. Alberich coughed a gout of fire at him, but Logi caught it and played with it—his own element.

Alberich reassumed his own shape. "What do you want?"

Logi repeated, "We came—we had to come to admire the miracles of your power. What you did is astonishing—impressive—I suppose. But you simply expanded—grew greater—puffed yourself up, as it were. Can you diminish?" Logi gestured with his hands, "Can you become small like, say, a toad?"

Alberich smiled, put on the helmet, and behold!—a toad.

Logi instantly stepped on it and began to crunch it. Alberich croaked and screamed. Logi took the toad between his fingers, squeezed it, and squeezed some more. Alberich pleaded for his life. "Yes," Logi said, "You can have your life if you give us the RhineGold—and the Tarnhelm, and—yes—the Ring." Alberich was silent; squeeze—"No!"—squeeze—"Yes! Yes!" Would Alberich swear by Votan's ashen spear? "Yes!" Done!

As soon as Logi had carved the bargain in fire on Votan's spear, he allowed Alberich to resume his form. Logi took the Tarnhelm, and handed it to Thor. Alberich had his dwarfs assemble the RhineGold, and Thor gathered it all into his cloak. Alberich turned away. There was silence.

"Begone!" Alberich shouted.

"And the Ring!" Logi whispered.

With a snarl, Alberich tore the Ring from his finger, extending it toward Thor. Votan stepped forward to seize it, but Alberich held on.

"Take it!" Alberich shouted, still holding on, "and take this curse with it: everyone will covet the Ring, and seek to destroy its owner in order to posses it. This curse I lay on it, I, who fashioned it."

Alberich released the Ring and dashed off pursued by his vengeful dwarfs, who had felt his power over them pass with the loss of the Ring.

In silence the gods rose from Nibelheim to Midgard weighted down with the RhineGold, Tarnhelm and Ring. The other gods and the giants, holding Freya, were assembled to conclude the contract.

Thor undid his cloak and spread out the RhineGold. It worked its magic on the giants who coveted the hoard at once. Fasolt demanded enough gold to hide Freya. The gods piled it up until Freya's body disappeared, but her hair shone, golden as the RhineGold itself. Seizing the Tarnhelm from Thor, Fafnir covered it. Then they all, giants and gods, walked around her. Fasolt pointed to a chink. Freya's blue eye peeped through.

"That is all there is," Votan claimed, turning away.

Fasolt pointed to the Ring, already feeling its power. Votan shook his head, but as he did so, the earth trembled, and Erda, the Power of the Earth, rose.

"Beware, Votan, Beware!" she cried pointing at him. The two ravens, Thought and Memory, flew from Votan's shoulders to settle on Erda, and three pairs of eyes glared at him. "Votan, the Ring will destroy you and all the gods!"

Votan stared back, and sensing the truth, he reluctantly placed the ring in the chink. As he did so, Erda vanished and the two ravens fluttered back to him.

The giants, happy with the Gold, shouted their agreement to that payment in place of Freya. She shook off the gold and rejoined the gods. Fasolt seized the Ring and placed it on his finger. The curse began its work at once; Fafnir seized his sledgehammer, donned the Tarnhelm to become invisible, and smashed Fasolt to death. The gods watched in appalled silence. Fafnir reappeared, tore the Ring from Fasolt's finger, placed it on his own, and strode off with the RhineGold.

All the gods turned then to gaze with pride and satisfaction on Valhalla their fortress of ice and cloud, glistening and glittering in the sky. Thor, with his thunder, fashioned a rainbow bridge leading to it, and one by one, two by two, they crossed over that rainbow bridge to the glory of their new home.

Below, far off, they heard the RhineMaidens pleading with Fafnir, "Give back the Gold!"

The Long Recovery

Days, months, years passed. Votan knew that he himself could not take the Ring. Somehow it would have to come to him as something he found, or as a gift.

Fafnir, in a forest cave, wearing Tarnhelm and Ring, took on the form of a dragon to guard the gold. Memory of the treasure was almost lost. Alberich, expelled by the dwarfs, wandered the earth, a creature of greed and malice, seeking to regain the ring. His brother Mime, who had fashioned the Tarnhelm, moved into the forest near Fafnir to set up a blacksmith shop. Votan, with his ravens, shunned the forest, but they were all mindful and remembered.

Time passed and the Ring remained hidden from sight.

On earth, in Midgard, Votan found the perfect instruments that he could manipulate in order to regain the Ring—humans. Just as he had used the giants to build Valhalla, now he planned to use humans to recover the Ring, yield it to him, and give him, Votan, dominion over all creation.

Assuming human form, Votan mingled with men as Velse, the Wolf.

He wedded one of their women, and started a tribe of hunters. When the tribe had grown in number, and become strong, swift, and self-sufficient, he left them, the Volsungs, children of Velse the Wolf, and returned to Asgard.

He left too soon, because later, in a forest skirmish with a neighboring tribe, the Volsungs were routed, and destroyed, with the exception of a boy and a girl. Siegmund, fleet of foot, escaped; his sister Sieglinde was seized by Hunding, chief of the enemy tribe, to become his wife.

He brought her to his home, a house built around a huge tree. That night, a one-eyed Wanderer with an ashen spear arrived claiming shelter until next day. As Hunding and the stranger talked, he rose and thrust a sword into that tree supporting the house, saying, "This sword is Nothung—Need. Whoever pulls this sword from the tree will find that this Need, Nothung, will answers his own need."

Then the Wanderer, not waiting for morning, left Hunding's home, disappearing as he walked through the door. Hunding grasped the sword but couldn't budge it.

A few years passed. Another stranger came to Hunding's house claiming shelter. In Hunding's absence, Sieglinde let him in, and they talked. They learned that they were both Volsungs. It was Siegmund! She told him about the sword in the tree. He plucked it out, but Sieglinde pleaded with him to replace it lest Hunding be angry at its loss. Siegmund did so as Hunding came home.

Hunding granted one night of hospitality, but in the morning, he warned, he and his people would hunt Siegmund to death like an animal.

Sieglinde fed Hunding his supper with a drugged drink which put him to sleep. Siegmund threw open the door. Moonlight and the intoxicating odors of spring, flooding the room, worked their magic on the two. Siegmund seized the sword, and the two of them, blinded by love, ran off into the forest.

Votan watched and hoped. When his two ravens were silent, he called his favorite daughter, Brunhilde, one of the nine Valkyries who rode the air seeking out the souls of heroes who died in battle. He instructed her, in the upcoming battle with Hunding, to save Siegmund and help him to escape with Sieglinde. Their child was going to be important to him.

Frikka, Votan's wife, overhearing the plan, was enraged. As the goddess of marriage, she claimed that both Siegmund and Sieglinde should die: she for leaving her husband, and he for betraying his trust as a house-guest. Votan and Frikka argued bitterly, but she was stating the law, and so he had to give in.

There was much he could have said about Siegmund and Sieglinde being his own descendants, but not at that moment to his wife, when she had the law on her side. So sadly and curtly he instructed Brunhilde to save Hunding and let Siegmund die.

Brunhilde flew from Valhalla down to the sleeping couple. She wakened Siegmund and told him he was to die by the will of the gods. He accepted but pleaded not for himself but for Sieglinde. Could Brunhilde save Sieglinde from the wrath of Hunding? Watching his bravery and his love, Brunhilde resolved to disobey her father and to save him.

In the distance Hunding's horn sounded, and shortly the two men joined combat. Brunhilde, working with her shield to save Siegmund, failed to notice the thunder and lightning with which Votan came. He smashed Nothung with his spear, and Siegmund fled followed by both Hunding and Votan.

Brunhilde picked up the shards of Nothung and hoisted Sieglinde onto her flying horse. The weeping Sieglinde wanted to know why she should live. With prophetic foresight, Brunhilde replied, "Because you will bear the greatest hero the world has seen." They flew to the Valkyrie's Rock where Brunhilde hoped to enlist help from her sisters before Voltan came to punish her.

THE EXPULSION OF BRUNHILDE FROM ASGARD

Back in the forest, cornered and weaponless, Siegmund fell before Hunding. Votan watched the death of the man whose life he had wanted to save. He thought of Frikka, and in rage, he struck Hunding dead. Then turning his mind to his disobedient daughter, he rode angrily off through the sky after her.

Up on the Valkyrie rock, Brunhilde persuaded her sister Valtraute to hide Sieglinde and the shards of the sword, Nothung. They agreed the best place would be with Mime, the blacksmith in the forest near Fafnir's cave, a place that Votan shunned. Then, deserted by her eight sisters, she stood alone to face her father.

Votan, flying in rage, arrived in sadness: he had to punish his favorite daughter. He began by pointing out his instructions and she nodded. When he had finished she replied softly, saying his first instruction had been to save Siegmund. She had followed the wishes of his heart, not the words of his mouth. Was he not satisfied with what she had tried to do?

He acknowledged sorrowfully what she said, but for her disobedience he had to strip her of her immortality. She made one final plea. Let him expel her from the gods and from Valhalla, but let him put her into a magic sleep there on the rock, surrounded with a fire that only the bravest hero in the world could pass through. Then let the hero's kiss waken her, no longer as a goddess, but as a woman.

Votan stood silent. The ravens Thought and Memory croaked assent. Votan kissed her on the forehead, and laid her in a shallow cave. Then he summoned the god of Fire: "Logi! Logi! Logi!"

With flickering fire Logi arrived and stood on the rock listening to Votan's instruction. Then as Logi surrounded the rock with a ring of magic flames that only the bravest man might pass through, Votan cast Brunhilde into an enchanted sleep from which only that bravest man might awaken her with a kiss.

SIEGFRIED

While Brunhilde slept within her ring of fire, and Fafnir the giant Dragon guarded his RhineGold, Mime kept jealous watch in the forest, hoping that someone—anyone—would kill the Dragon. He lusted after the Tarnhelm, the Ring, and all the RhineGold. That had been his dream for age on age. In his blacksmith shop lived Siegfried, the son of Sieglinde who had died. Mime watched Siegfired hopefully. Was this his instrument to destroy Fafnir?

Many times over the years, Mime had tried to re-forge the shards of the magic sword Nothung. He failed each time because, at the end, he lacked the power and the fire to melt and temper it.

When Siegfried reached adulthood, he grew exasperated with the incompetence of Mime, and working both bellows and hammer, he re-forged the magic sword himself. Mime's eyes glowed with greed. He told Siegfried about Fafnir and the Gold, but only that much, saying nothing of the Tarnhelm or the Ring. He led Siegfried a few miles to the Dragon's lair, and proposed a plan he had hatched over ages of thought. The two of them dug a pit in the Dragon's path, and Mime coached Siegfried in the sword-thrust upward to the dragon's heart, the sword-thrust that would kill Fafnir. When everything was ready, Siegfried leaped into the pit and blew his horn.

Fafnir slid out of his cave in clouds of smoke and flame, no longer the active giant, but a slow-moving Dragon. As he crawled over the pit, Siegfried watched for the pulsing heart and thrust Nothung upward. In the writhing death of the giant, no longer a serpent, Siegfried was unhurt but covered with blood. When he licked his lips and hands, all his senses were sharpened: smells were stronger, sounds were clearer, and taste was keener. Suddenly he could understand birds and animals!

They sang to him that Mime was preparing a poisoned drink for him. Contemptuously Siegfried slashed off Mime's head. Then the animals told him of the Tarnhelm, of the RhineGold, and of the Ring. Siegfried removed the Tarnhelm from the dead giant's head, and took the ring from the giant's finger. Walking back into the cave he found the gold. Siegfried was too naïve and simple for the use of those treasures. For him the Gold was a pretty lump, the Tarnhelm a toy, and the Ring a trinket.

A forest bird sang of a beautiful woman sleeping on a rock inside a ring of fire. That was something Siegfried could understand. Leaving the gold in the cave, he set off wearing both Tarnhelm and Ring. When he walked by the river, he heard three voices singing of gold, but he didn't understand their song.

Following the forest bird along the Rhine, Siegfried came to the path leading up to the Valkyrie rock and climbed. At the first turn, he found his way barred by a one-eyed stranger with a black raven on each shoulder. Siegfried ordered the stranger out of his way. When the stranger raised his ashen spear to forbid passage, Siegfried drew Nothung and hewed the spear in two.

Votan disappeared into thin air, troubled and fearful that all the covenants, contracts, and vows carved onto the staff in runes were now invalidated by the destruction of the spear. He looked at his two ravens and recalled the warning Erda had given, "Beware, Votan! The Ring will destroy you and all the gods." In his wisdom he knew that he could no longer control or manipulate the movement of the Ring; its power had passed to Siegfried.

Unaware of the destruction he had caused by hewing the spear, Siegfried climbed on. When he came to the magic fire, he walked through it without a pause, entered the cave, and claimed Brunhilde with a kiss. She awoke, as she had requested, to the bravest man in the world. To her surprise, she was subject to him, having lost her immortality and her powers as a goddess. This was difficult for her. She found Siegfried's innocence and simplicity difficult to accept, but she gradually grew happy in her new-found love. Each evening they sat on their cliff overlooking the Rhine. They heard far off the dolorous wail of the RhineMaidens. Siegfried didn't understand their grief; Brunhilde did, but said nothing.

Days and weeks passed. Siegfried grew irritable and restless. Brunhilde, all too mortal now, saw that he would have to leave in order to return to her. She agreed he should go on a Rhine journey in exchange for his promise to return to their circle of fire. Sad at parting, but eager to go, he gave her the Ring as a token for his return. Then he built a boat, and with the Tarnhelm, he took off up the Rhine. When the RhineMaidens saw no Ring on his finger, they were silent.

THE VICTIMS OF THE RING

Just as Votan had begotten a son through whom he hoped to regain the Ring, so Alberich, the Ring-maker, had begotten a son, Hagen, on Krimhild, a beautiful mortal, and then deserted her. Later she married the King of the Gibichungs, and bore him two children, Gunther and Gutrune. When Gunther became king, they all three lived together in their castle on the Rhine.

Alberich visited Hagen in dreams, and foretold Siegfried's approach.

In clear sunlight and fragrant air, Siegfried sailed up the Rhine for three days. In the moonlight of the third night he came to a castle. Guiding his boat to it, he tied up at a wharf, and stepped ashore, where he was challenged. Tall, with black hair and dark eyes that sparkled in the moonlight, Hagen questioned Siegfried who answered fearlessly, simply, and without guile. When he had heard all Segfried could tell, Hagen led him, with courtly politeness, to his own wing of the castle, promising to present him to the King of the Gibichungs next day.

Hagen had many things to ponder. Siegfried was not wearing the Ring, but carried the Tarnhelm slung at his waist. While Siegfried slept, Alberich came to Hagen in dream again to devise a plan for the recovery of the treasures.

When Siegfried awoke, Hagen gave him wine containing a potion of forgetfulness, and Siegfried lost all memory for everything—the trip, Brunhilde, the Gold, the Dragon, and Mime. Siegfried knew only what Hagen told him, and Hagen knew a lot since Siegfried had answered all questions fearlessly, simply, and without guile. When presented to Gunther and Gutrune, he told a simple tale of youth looking for adventure, and he shone like a golden star. Gutrune was attracted, and while they flirted together, Hagen and Gunther plotted. They entertained Siegfried with joust and hunt for three days. When Siegfried asked to marry Gutrune, Gunther granted the request with one simple condition.

Three days downstream was a high rock, all on fire. Legend said a beautiful blond blue-eyed maiden slept in the flames. If Siegfried could claim the maiden as Gunther's bride, then he could marry Gutrune. Siegfried accepted immediately and was eager to start. Gunther suggested they prepare for a day, and Hagen taught Siegfried two of the uses of the Tarnhelm: to travel instantly wherever he chose, and to assume the form of Gunther so that the maiden would think Gunther had brought her from the flames. Siegfried, pleased and surprised by the power of his helmet, readily agreed to the plan.

After three days on the river, they arrived at the foot of the fiery rock. Siegfried, donning the Tarnhelm to look like Gunther, climbed the height and passed through the flames at dusk. Brunhilde was appalled. Who was this dark stranger who came through the flames? Siegfried, more mature now than he had been when he left, demanded the Ring, and set his sword between himself and Brunhilde to guard her till their wedding day. The next morning he led her to the boat, handing her over to Gunther's attendants. Then Siegfried, in the Tarnhelm, transported himself magically to the Gibichung castle and to Gutrune.

Two days later, Hagen gathered the Gibichungs in great solemnity to welcome Gunther and his bride. At her arrival, Brunhilde, on Gunther's arm, greeted the Gibichungs civilly. When she looked about, she was astonished to see Siegfried.

"Hold!" she cried. Advancing to stand before him, she said, "This is my husband." Siegfried stared unbelieving.

"Months ago this man came through the flames and claimed me as his bride." Siegfried shook his head in denial.

She called for a spear, and Hagen offered his. With her hand on the shaft, she swore that Siegfried, months previously, had come through the flames and claimed her. Siegfried, placing his hand on the shaft, swore that he had not, adding that he hoped the weapon would kill him if he lied. Never taking her oath hand from the blade, Brunhilde pointed to the Ring on Siegfried's finger, saying "Gunther took that ring from me four nights ago. Why isn't it on his finger now?"

His hand still on the shaft, Siegfried lied, "I have never seen you before."

Brunhilde looked first at Gunther and saw his uneasiness at not having the Ring; she looked at Hagen and saw his rage that Siegfried had the Ring; she looked at Gutrune and saw the reflection of her own love for Siegfried; finally looking at Siegfried, she saw only simple earnestness. Lifting her hand from the sword, she pointed to him saying quietly, "Liar and traitor," before she walked slowly over to place her hand in Gunther's once more.

Gunther announced that in two days, two weddings would be celebrated: his own and his sister's. But the next day, the entire court would hunt. In general discomfort and unease, they all retired to the castle. The only person feeling no discomfort or unease was Siegfried.

At the hunt next day, the parties separated, and Siegfried wandered alone by the river. The RhineMaidens, drawn by the Ring, came up and tried to coax it from him. He joked pleasantly with them, but they fell silent and swam away as Hagen came to lead Siegfried to the outdoor court. Hoping to kill Siegfried and take the Rings for his father, Hagen gave him a potion to restore his memory. As they joined Gunther with his retinue, Hagen said, "Tell us more, Siegfried, more about yourself." Siegfried began to talk.

He told of his youth in the forest with Mime, of re-forging his father's magic sword, of the Dragon with the hoard, of fighting Fafnir, of understanding birds, and of learning about the rock crowned with fire. As he talked Gutrune and Brunhilde approached and listened. He told of climbing the mountain and meeting the one-eyed Stranger with the two ravens whose spear he had broken. Brunhilde heard this with horror, knowing that all Votan's treaties and covenants were now void. Then he told of passing through the fire and claiming Brunhilde, his bride.

When Siegfried saw Brunhilde and started toward her, arms outstretched in love, Hagen, from behind, stabbed him with his spear. "He betrayed King Gunther," Hagen said, pulling out his bloody spear, "and in his oath yeserday, he asked for this spear to kill him if he lied."

Brunhilde strode forward pointing at Hagen and shouting, "Liar and traitor—traitor to your king, Gunther, traitor to Siegfried, and traitor to me!" Gunther signaled for his men to surround Hagen.

Brunhilde laid Siegfried's sword on his body, drew his cloak about him, and walked by his side as Gunther's vassals bore him back to the castle.

The Tiumph of the Ring

In the courtyard, Brunhilde ordered Gunther's men to build a funeral pyre and to lay Siegfried on it. Hagen, breaking loose as he passed the pyre, tried to leap up and tear the Ring from Siegfried's hand, but the dead hand rose and clenched its fist to deny him. He fell back terrified, and was led off to execution.

Brunhilde mounted the wooden pile to stand beside Siegfried. She told them all the long tale of Siegfried, descendant of gods, and then of herself, daughter of gods. Then she lit the funeral pyre for her own immolation with Siegfried.

While the pyre burned, the castle burst into flames. The rainbow bridge to Valhalla faded. Valhalla, the fortress of ice and cloud, blew away in rising winds. Its foundations of ice melted, flooding Midgard. The sky filled with clouds. The gods were blinded, lost in mist. Yggdrasil, the World Tree, whipped loose: branches snapped in Asgard, the trunk in Midgard bent and split, and the roots in Nibelheim shook free as the earth trembled. The caves of the dwarfs collapsed burying them. Mountains tumbled, hills slid into valleys, men and giants were shaken to death, and as the seas rose over their shores, animals and plants drowned.

The Rhine flooded the Hall of the Gibichungs. The RhineMaidens swam into the hall and seized the Ring. At last, the Gold would be theirs again.

Then all the land drowned until the whole world was one wide ocean. Once more, there was only water.

THE END

KEY TO PRONUNCIATION IN THE RING OF THE NIBELUNGEN

Aesir	**ay**-seer (ay as in say)
Alberich	**al**-buh-reek
Brunhilde	**broon**-heel-duh
Erda	**air**-duh
Fafnir	**faff**-neer
Fasolt	**fa**-soult
Freya	**fray**-uh
Frikka	**frick**-uh (as in sick)
Gibichungs	**gee**-bee-chungs (u as in put)
Grimhild	**greem**-heeld
Gunther	**goon**-tear (u as in put)
Gutrune	goo-**troon**-uh
Hagen	**haw**-gn
Hunding	**hun**-ding (u as in put)
Logi	**low**-gee (hard g as in good)
Mime	**mee**-muh
Nibelheim	**nee**-buhl-hime (as in time)
Nibelungen	**nee**-buh-lung-en (hard g, and lung has u as in put)

Siegfried	**seeg**-freed
Sieglinde	**seeg**-lin-duh
Siegmund	**seeg**-moond
Valhalla	val-**hal**-uh
Valkyrie	**val**-kee-ree
Valtraute	**val-trow**-tuh (double accent)
Velse	**vell**-suh
Volsungs	**vole**-soongs
Votan	**voe**-tawn
Yggdrasil	**ig**-druh-sill (ig as in pig)

Sacha: Artist

INTRODUCTION TO SACHA ARTIST

What is the nature of the reality in artistic creation? What, for example, is the relation of the world created by Tolkien to us and to our world? And what is the relation between a portrait by Rembrandt with the model and with the viewer?

This story examines those problems posed to the artist, to those who view the art, and to the models for the artist.

1

From the time she could hold a pencil, Sacha would draw. At first it was tiny rows of symmetrical circles. Later, she graded them from small to large and back. Before starting school, she was drawing pictures. So with no training, she understood, from intuition and practice, two of drawing's fundamental elements: *Line* and *Shape.*

Later, she had weekly art lessons from Yvonne Ernst, and loved both the teacher and the subject. The addition of *Balance* gave a stillness to her work. *Perspective* with its attention to background, middleground, and foreground gave depth to her drawing and focused a viewer on her subject. Then came *color* with its theory of primary and complementary elements. They all led inevitably to *Focus,* and finally to *Harmony* which gave her drawing and painting a completeness not visible before. Her own *Dynamism* was her gift to art itself.

"Whose *Focus* and whose *Harmony* are we talking about?" Sacha asked her teacher.

"Mine! Whose else?" Yvonne replied unabashedly.

Within a year of two, however, Sacha's own taste dictated all seven elements, and Yvonne expressed satisfaction, even when disagreeing.

Her family and art teachers praised Sacha's mastery of the elements, obvious from the reality in her drawings. But they all agreed that her amazing personal quality was the vividness of her renderings—the feeling that a viewer was looking here and now at the real thing.

Her progress through pencil, charcoal, watercolor, and oil was like a seamless and effortless development. Her great synthesis came after hours, weeks, months, and years of practice with the individual elements—*Line, Shape, Balance, Perspective, Color, Focus,* and *Harmony*—in all and various combinations. That synthesis led to a mastery of her medium. *Dynamism*, as was stated, was her gift to art. It was a quality of her own personality projected into her art.

Often the act of drawing became, somehow, a reproduction of some image in her mind. It was eerie to watch her work. She looked off into some private distance, and then drew. She looked off again for a time, and then continued to draw. It was as if she saw something in fantasy or in memory and drew it, not from the life, but from her mind or memory.

When she was twelve, she stopped her lessons with Yvonne, who said to the family, "If I stay any longer, she'll be teaching me." As a parting gift, Yvonne gave her a box of aquarelle pencils. With them she could draw in color with or without water. They were like a triple gift: she could use them simply as colored pencils, or she could wet the pencils and get shining color that looked like oil paint, or she could draw in colored pencil and add a water wash to blur it into watercolor. With the aquarelles she drew with a vitality that she achieved in no other medium.

Sacha was justifiably proud of her skill, and in her backyard one afternoon she sketched a dinner-plate dahlia with the wet aquarelles—quilled red outer petals with a white circle around the yellow center. Her brother was dribbling a soccer ball when he wasn't staring at Sacha's work. Once his ball struck Sacha's foot, and jolted her hand.

"I'm sorry, Sacha," Max called.

"No problem," she said as she took an eraser to rub out the fault in the drawing.

"Sacha, look!" Max cried. Where Sacha had erased the center of the flower, the center of the real flower disappeared and all the petals fell to the ground.

"Big problem!" Sacha cried, pointing to the petals.

"Rub out the rest of the flower, and see what happens," Max suggested.

When she rubbed out the stem, the real stem disappeared. When she rubbed out the bit of grass behind the plant, the grass disappeared and there was bare earth.

"Wow, Max," she said, "this is too scary!" White-faced, she packed up the aquarelles, threw out the water, and went into the house.

After supper she told her story, looking at no one, speaking in a flat voice, and looking frightened.

"Let's go and see what happened," her mother said, and led the family out to see the dahlia—nothing now but a circle of red petals on a patch of bare earth.

"Draw another flower—that one—but just draw the flower," Sacha's mother said,

"I'll get water for you, Sacha," Max said, as Sacha went for her aquarelles.

When the two returned, Sacha set up her easel, and sketched the flower with the aquarelles under the eyes of the family. The water dried quickly.

"Now, rub it out," her mother said. Sacha rubbed it out, petal by petal, but the garden flower stood up jauntily, immune to the eraser.

"Let's go and think about this," her mother said, leading the way indoors.

By "think" of course, her mother meant "talk". Were those the crayons? Was the water applied before or after the drawing? Was the sun shining? Which way was she facing? And so on. Nothing relevant came from the discussion.

But next morning, Sacha remembered! She had been in a hurry and used rainwater that she scooped out of the birdbath. The experiments began. She worked with rainwater and found it frightening to watch things disappear. Boiled tap water wouldn't work. Demineralized water (treated water)

wouldn't work either. Distilled water worked perfectly. They tried adding grains of salt, and after a couple of grains, the distilled water wouldn't work either.

Sacha put away the aquarelles in her art cupboard. "What I can do with them is too frightening for me," she explained.

A few weeks later, Max watched Sacha as she drew a mermaid. He asked, "When you draw a mermaid, does a mermaid come into existence?"

"There are no such things as mermaids," Sacha said dismissively.

"But when you draw them, do you create them? I know that's the reverse of destroying what you draw, but do they come into existence?" Max persisted.

"Why talk about mermaids?" Sacha replied. "Why not cats? Why don't I draw a cat?" She set up her easel in the dining room, and went to get the aquarelles. She drew the dining room floor, and a golden cat using the aquarelle colored pencils. When she gave a water wash, a cat appeared on the floor.

The two housecats, MJ and LL, rose on their claws. Hissing, they leaped toward the new cat who looked around helplessly. Sacha grabbed the cat into her arms, while Max rubbed with the eraser. Nothing happened. The two house cats crouched to leap up on Sacha as she took the eraser from Max, set the cat on her shoulders, and rubbed out the drawing. The cat disappeared, along with a bit of the mat.

"I guess if you draw something, only you can destroy it by erasing it. You've got some great power, Sacha," Max said in awe.

Sacha quickly re-drew the floor she had destroyed, murmuring, "I wish I didn't have it."

"Then stop using distilled water," Max advised pragmatically.

Later, Max raised other questions. "Where did the cat and the flowers go when Sacha erased them?" To the family, Sacha confessed her feeling that she had destroyed them.

"What if they went into another dimension? or into a parallel universe?" Max asked.

"I think it's very simple," Sacha said. "When I rub them out, they never existed."

"What about the mat?"

"That's the scary part. I'm not going to think about it, but I believe when I draw something using distilled water, somehow, I gain physical power over it."

The aquarelles sat in her art cupboard until she left home.

2

When she graduated from high school, Sacha was accepted at the Rhode Island School of Design, and moved from Calgary in western Canada to Providence, Rhode Island in the United States. What a different geography and culture! She moved from the mountains to the sea, and from formal politeness to almost anarchic informality.

The first year she lived in residence, and found herself chafing at the absence of order or rules. She did all her study at the library where she could organize her thoughts.

In her second year she moved into an apartment with two classmates, Rachel Newman and Eilleen Burke. At the apartment, Rachel and Sacha expected to be caretakers for Eilleen who was legally blind, but they found that their services were unnecessary. Though she carried the white cane of blindness, Eilleen saw perfectly up close, and was a gifted miniaturist.

In the spring of that second year, a masked man tried to snatch Eilleen's knapsack outside the library when it closed. Eilleen fought back, and shouted, drawing the attention of many students who saw her white cane waving. As the students ran toward them, Eilleen freed her arm with the cane, smacked the man over the head, and scratched his face tearing off the mask. He fled.

The police came, and when the detective saw Eilleen's cane, he sighed, rolled his eyes, and said, "We usually ask people to identify their assailant. Can you tell us anything?"

"Yes," Eilleen said, "he was a white male a few inches taller than me, with dark hair, and expensive dark clothes. His fingerprints are on my cane because he tried to take it. He'll have a lump on his head and a deep scratch on his face. I can make a drawing of him."

"But I thought you were blind," the detective said.

"I'm legally blind, but I can see distinctly up close, and I was certainly up close to him."

At the police station, Eilleen sketched and colored a miniature of her assailant. When the picture appeared in the paper the next morning with a shot of Eilleen standing with her cane, many people identified him, and the police had arrested him by noon the same day. He was from a moderately wealthy family, but he was a gambler and needed more money than his family wanted to provide. The family engaged, a good attorney to defend him, and the case came up for trial the following week.

Several other people who had reported being mugged identified him also, and the police were pleased to have the perpetrator of many unsolved muggings in their custody.

The charge was assault and battery. In the court room, moving up close to him, Eilleen verified his identification. Many of her classmates and the families of other victims crowded into the courtroom to watch. Sacha was there drawing pictures of the people involved. First she drew Eilleen with her lawyer. Then she drew the defendant with his lawyer. She sketched the room itself and the Judge. Then she colored the main ones with her aquarelles. There they were—the main protagonists—in living color, and many in the court asked for copies.

The trial progressed well, and Eilleen's case seemed iron-clad. But when the defense lawyer, an expert defense attorney, asked Eilleen to identify the defendant from across the courtroom, Eilleen couldn't see him clearly. The lawyer stressed the need for identification *beyond all reasonable doubt*. Eilleen's lawyer pointed to the accuracy of Eilleen's drawing, the scratch on the defendant's face, and her identification from up close. But for the jury, a seed of reasonable doubt was planted. After a short deliberation, the jury found the defendant Not Guilty.

The art students in the gallery and the families of other victims were appalled by what they saw as a miscarriage of justice. The defendant and his lawyer were triumphant. The man laughed across the court pointing at Eilleen.

With her aquarelles, Sacha quickly sketched more scratches across his face and reddened the lawyer's face. Silence fell in the court. Everyone saw the marks of shame on both the perpetrator and his lawyer. The two of them were ignorant of those changes, but they found out quickly that they were marked for life, the one with scratches, and other with a permanent blush. Later, Sacha burned the pictures. The changes on their faces were now irreversible.

Max called a few days later and said, "You drew them with the aquarelles, didn't you?"

"I sure did," Sacha grated, "and I've burned the pictures. Nothing can undo the marks."

During her third year Sacha dated Michael Driscoll, an engineering student at Brown University in the Officer Training Course with the Army. The relationship became serious, and they lived together through Sacha's fourth year. She graduated with high honors, and became engaged to Michael. They planned to get married in the autumn of that year before Michael's first posting abroad.

At home for that final summer alone, Sacha became obsessed with the question Max had asked years before: where did the objects go when she erased them? When Max visited for two weeks, she asked him the question.

"Years ago," he replied, "you claimed you had destroyed them. Do you still think so?"

"I don't. And I wouldn't be asking the question if I still thought so."

"Why don't you draw a picture of yourself and rub it out?"

"That's what I'm afraid to do. How do I bring myself back if I disappear?"

"Then draw two pictures of yourself, exactly the same, and rub one out."

Sacha drew the pictures quickly and colored them with the aquarelles. When she rubbed the first one out, the second picture disappeared.

"Sacha, try something different," Max murmured. "Draw a picture of yourself with paper and aquarelles and a clock set at 3. Then draw another one with the clock set twenty minutes later, and tomorrow at 3, rub out the first starting with the pad and aquarelles, so that if you disappear, you can either wait until 3:20 to see if you come back, or draw yourself back."

Sacha thought it over and said, "I'll add a calendar of this month. Be here at 3 tomorrow afternoon and we'll try."

By 3 the next day she had two parallel drawings, one with the clock set at 3, and one with the clock set at 3:20. Max came early, and on the stroke of 3 she erased the first drawing, starting at the aquarelles and the pad. Max leaped to his feet.

That was the last thing she saw in the real world.

In that other world, she stood in dazzling light. Everything near her was in vivid color; everything a few feet from her was mist-wrapped, almost invisible. It was a silent world of sight. No other senses were involved—no sound, smell, taste, or, she realized with amazement, no sense of touch.

Where did the light come from? Nothing above or around explained it. No shadows. The light came from the place itself.

"It's like television without sound," she whispered. It sounded like a shout in that stillness. She could see clearly everything near her. There were pictures she had drawn before, and the dahlia—and the cat! It mewed silently and rubbed against her ankles. She bent over to stroke it. She couldn't feel it! The sight of it rubbing against her ankles had "caused" her to feel it there. "How often does one sense create another?" she asked herself.

She examined the other pictures. Everything she had drawn with the aquarelles and erased stood near her bathed in brightness. There were no shadows because the light came from her own artwork.

She took a step away from the cat, and everything she faced started to move toward her—giant shadowy buildings, statues, vague forms. She trembled. What was happening? She stepped back toward the cat. The moving things stopped. She gripped her pencils and paper and tried to draw herself. Could she get back? She had no sense of touch, and had to depend completely on sight. Her hands trembled, and she tried to concentrate, but she couldn't feel herself drawing, and everything was in slow motion.

Suddenly she was back in the real world with Max.

The clock showed 3:20.

He gasped, "I'm so relieved. Where were you?"

"Max, first of all, let's burn that other picture so that I won't disappear again." They took the picture outside, and set it alight.

When he returned, she said, "I was in a world where everything I had drawn was distinct, but beyond that everything was shadowy, and I was afraid to move."

"Could you see me? Could you see this real world?" Max asked.

"No, nothing! Where I was, everything I had drawn and rubbed out was distinct, and in color. The cat was there, like I said, and rubbed against me. The dahlia center was still fresh. But everything else around me was grey and misty. When I moved, everything I looked at came toward me through the mist."

"Did you move around?"

"A little, but I was afraid to. I started to draw myself back, but at 3:20, the other picture drew me back."

"Thank god you had the other picture with a different time!"

"I won't do that again!" Sacha vowed, and returned the aquarelles to her cupboard.

3

Sacha and Michael were married, and lived in Germany for two years. They were then posted to Alaska for three years, and Sacha was able to visit her parents in Calgary. When they were posted to Virginia, they stayed for ten years. They had three children, one at each posting. She and Michael called little Mike their German child, and Norah was their Alaskan child. Nick, the last, was their Virginian.

Sacha's art was acclaimed at first nation-wide and then world-wide. The precise qualities that had first astonished people—vitality and vividness—continued to astonish them. After ten years in Virginia, Michael was posted half a world away to teach for one year. For the first time, Sacha didn't go with him, but stayed with the children in Virginia.

The Department of Recruitment at the Pentagon made Sacha an offer—to produce posters for an enlistment campaign. It would mean a commitment either to traveling or to living in Washington, but the job paid well, and she could sign the posters. Before accepting, she discussed it with Michael by phone, and talked over all the implications with the children at the kitchen table.

Her oldest son, fifteen-year-old Mike, the image of his father with the dark hair and dark eyes, wanted a military career like his father, and was in favor of the contract. Her daughter Norah, a 13-year-old pacifist, argued with her brother Michael and tried to discourage her mother from accepting the contract. The brother and sister looked so alike that Sacha had to laugh. "Oil and water," she thought. Nick, the youngest, looked like Sacha. He couldn't speak strongly for or against, but didn't want to change schools. They were interrupted by a knock at the door, and Nick went to answer.

He came rushing back shouting "Oh, mom!" as a Colonel walked into the room.

"Could I see you alone?" he asked Sacha.

With a sinking heart, Sacha remained in her chair at the kitchen table, and waved the three children to other chairs. Though her heart was racing and she felt weak, she said evenly, "Anything you have to say, we'll hear as a family."

"Well, I have very bad news for you. Your husband was killed in the line of duty today, and we came at once to tell you."

"In the line of duty!" Sacha gasped, leaping up. "We aren't at war! How could he . . . . ?"

"It was friendly fire," the Colonel said reassuringly.

"What do you mean, 'friendly fire'?"

"He was teaching a combat course, and one of the younger men accidentally shot him."

"Why did they have live ammunition?" Sacha shouted.

"We don't know. We have many questions ourselves, and will do a full and thorough investigation into all the circumstances. When we have finished, we will give you a report on the results of our investigation. Meanwhile, I am here to tell you how he was killed and to offer sincere official condolences."

Sacha looked around stunned. Had this man really reported what she had heard? And had he actually said "sincere official condolences"? She saw the shock on the faces of her children. She stretched out her arms, pulling them to her gently. "Thank you" she said. "I have lots of questions but I'll ask them later. Thank you for coming. Please let yourself out."

As the door closed, she gave a scream and hugged all the children to her for a long time. Grief erased every reasonable thought: the contract was forgotten.

Three months later, the Department of Public Relation at the Pentagon approached her to consider the same contract. The previous offer had come from the Department of Recruitment.

"Why is the contract now with Public Relations and not Recruitment?" she asked.

"With you as a survivor of a military death, we felt this would look better."

"Look better to whom?" Sacha snapped.

"Better to the public," was the prompt reply.

"Give me a week to think," Sacha said, letting them out the door.

She discussed it with the children, and sounded inclined to accept.

"Mom, how could you do this after . . . . ?" Norah whispered.

"Trust me, darling, it will all be fine," Sacha responded. But she knew there was something she needed to do—something she needed to know—before she could accept the contract, and for that knowledge, she needed her brother Max.

She called Max that night. He wasn't in. She left a message for him to call her next day at his convenience. When he called, she began her business at once. "Do you remember when I drew myself at two different times, and rubbed out the first drawing? You were there keeping guard."

"Yes, and I remember how spooky it was for me, not knowing whether or not you would come back."

"I want to do that again, but I want to be gone an hour this time. I need you because you're the only one who understands what happens when I use the aquarelles.

"I may not be able to come for a week," Max said. "Could one of the children keep watch if you need to know quickly?"

"I'm very touchy about telling anyone about the aquarelles. I feel like a witch, with 'strange powers', and I don't want the children to be afraid of me. I don't have to explain anything to you, and I would really appreciate it if you could come out for a weekend? I'll get everything ready."

"I'll arrive a week from Friday night. I'm still a little bit afraid of it. Are you sure it will work out?"

"I haven't used them for a long time, but trust me. This will work."

Saturday morning at 10:00, Max sat in her studio with his cell phone turned off, and the phone extension in the studio unplugged. He gave full attention to what was happening in that room.

Sacha had made a drawing of herself in the studio exactly as she was dressed that morning with a clock set prominently at 10:00 beside a calendar. There was another painting, identical except for the time: 11:00. At 10:00 she rubbed out the first drawing, and disappeared. The last thing she heard was Max's gasp of fear and surprise.

This time she noticed the suddenness with which she left the real world and entered this "other" world. "From my point of view, the flower I first drew disappeared petal by petal, but from the flower's point of view, it must have been sudden and total." She wondered whether there was yet another world—a partial-between one—but had no time to think.

She remembered the bubble of brilliant light around everything she had drawn and erased. Beside her were the original dahlia and the golden cat. She crouched down to look more closely. Yes. It was that cat, mewing silently, still alive and unchanged—and the dahlia center was still fresh. Beyond the light was the grey foggy world. Shapes loomed just out of sight in the mist.

She took a step. Everything hidden in the mist moved slowly toward her. With another step everything moved more quickly. She stepped back beside the cat. All movement stopped.

She walked forward into the greyness. Shapes came toward her through space—now the ruins of a great cathedral engulfed her, now an unfinished open-air theater passed through her. The farther she moved, the faster the art objects passed by and through her, all incomplete or flawed.

She controlled the speed by moving back toward the cat—her personal space. Over there was a half-finished Stonehenge-like circle; over there was something she had only heard rumors about, the *Weeping Mona Lisa.* A flood of objects flowed toward her and past her. There was a small roughly-hewn statue of *David* by Michelangelo, and some half-finished paintings by Raphael

She figured it out. This was the land of artistic creations never completed. That was why they were hidden from her. They had existed only in truncated form and never finished. They had been only partially drawn or painted, imperfectly sculpted or etched, written down incompletely, or never fully built. Except the cat!—and the dahlia! Somehow her stuff was different!

Wherever she turned, everything moved toward her. She felt confused. Why did everything move toward her eyes from whatever direction, wherever she looked? Here a statue, there a painting or a manuscript, all indistinct.

She stood near the cat, and stared ahead. The procession of artistic things moved slowly. Picassos and Monets rolled toward her. She turned a little to the right, and Dali and Miro came at her. The longer she looked, the farther back in time she went. She took a step. Products from Italy and Egypt streamed toward her. Then came the Middle East—a ziggurat, incomplete hanging gardens—then ruins like Angkor Wat. Turning left she saw Viking shields, half-built dragon-ships.

"I must be looking east," she said, and turned around. Now kontiki-like figures floated at her—pagodas, models of Shinto shrines.

She stumbled to the cat again. In the bright light all movement stopped. Once again vague shapes hovered in the mist. "They all start from the recent past," she murmured to herself. "When I move toward them, a procession of things from the past come in succession. If I stood here long enough, I could see the whole history of art and architecture around the world!" She turned south.

Nothing happened.

She stepped away from the cat, and pre-Columbian art with pyramids and feathered statues, Inca gold, emeralds, and knotted cords floated toward her.

She got lost watching history roll backward. She heard nothing.

Why couldn't she hear music or songs that were never finished? The answer came in a flash. Her own creativity was visual, and her talent and genius trapped her in a visual world. Her view in this other world would always be limited to her own creative gift—visual art. She felt anxious but she made herself relax. The other painting would pull her back wherever she was in that silent world. She turned about aimlessly, having lost interest once she had figured out what was hidden there.

Now she had the answer to the question that had drawn her to this world again. The cat didn't die; it lived eternally the same. And the dahlia center never dried out. These gave the answers she had hoped for. People she erased didn't die. Like the cat, they lived forever in that silent world. They were trapped in that silent world—true—but they lived. Maybe they could hear the cat and each other . . . .

Suddenly she was back in the real world, in her real home, with her brother gasping in relief.

"Thank god you're back; I was frantic with worry.

"Most of it was the way I remembered," she explained. "I was less anxious, and could notice more. I think it's a land of the Muses—a place where everything imagined but not shaped or written down exists. The cat is still alive and mewing, but I couldn't hear it. And that original dahlia is still fresh after all these years."

"Was there music too? Did you hear any unwritten songs?"

"There was no sound. The only sense for me was sight, but then I'm totally visual. I was aware only of what I could see. I didn't notice anything else."

"Did you learn anything you can use?"

"Yes. What I erase goes to that land where it lives—or at least doesn't die."

"Will it disappear when the person who created it or imagined it dies?

"I'll never know. I saw lots of creations, but no people. Only the cat was alive. I don't feel guilty for rubbing out people; they aren't really destroyed."

"They're dead to this world," Max pointed out.

"I know," Sacha said, "but they're alive over there."

Sacha turned away, and Max could see that she was miles away in thoughts of her own.

"Does that clear the way for something you're planning?" Max asked.

"Maybe." Sacha met his glance and continued, "I'm not sure. But I couldn't have learned what I needed to know if you hadn't come."

"Did this have anything to do with Mike's death. Is there some connection that you're not telling me about?"

"I don't think so," Sacha said. "It has more to do with the contract the Pentagon wants to offer me, but even then, the connections aren't clear to me. But Max, I had to do this." She fell silent. "I'll promise you this. If there are connections that develop, I'll tell you."

Max knew that he would learn nothing more. "I'm hungry," he said. "Let's eat!" They moved to the kitchen.

4

Her posters for army, navy, air force, and marines were dazzling, and she was invited to the Pentagon to meet with people from the Enlistment Department. As they praised the posters, Sacha shrugged. "I could have produced better ones for you," she said.

"What do you mean? They're wonderful and the response has been great."

"True," Sacha said, "but the posters lack the quality that would get people to join up in droves. They lack romantic context."

"Do you mean men and women . . . . ?"

"No. I mean mystery, excitement, and the romance of faraway places. The posters I just finished focus on patriotism and opportunity for education. I want to put models on ships, tanks, and submarines, to suggest travel and a carefree life."

"Why didn't you tell us?"

"Wait," said Sacha. "I've been happy to work for you, but you have to admit that this is my first opportunity to give suggestions. So far, I've just obeyed orders. Now I would plead with you to think about locations. A marine in no recognizable place like the one in that poster is nothing compared to a marine at an island base with palm trees and clouds. That would intrigue rabid pacifists."

"Could you do it with photographs?"

"No. I've tried it. You know that I make things more real than reality itself with soul and vitality when I work in the actual setting. When I'm actually there, that is when I do my best work. Here's what I propose. Assign me a man and woman from each service—army, navy, air force, marines, and coastguard—you left them out—and then let's look at bases all over the world. Fly us to the sites. I could draft the stuff in a few days, and produce them after we returned home again."

"How many would you propose?"

"How many bases do you have? Remember, the exotic and unusual will appeal to many people, but there are some who like the familiar. And if I may make a particular point, I want the public to get to know these ten people that I draw. It's better for them to see the same people in different setting to give the sense of travel."

At home, she and her children agreed that the three of them should go to live with their uncle Max and his family. With that settled, Sacha was ready for work.

The Departments of Recruitment and of Public Relations at the Pentagon were thrilled by her suggestions. The ten chosen service people quickly bonded into an acting team quite at ease singly or with any of the others in posing. Sacha, at each location, spent time with the people drawing them on site. At the same time, she quietly made aquarelle drawings of the bases with distilled water, but without personnel, and with no particular plan.

She came home after five months of travel and work, and the children joined her. She carried on with the paintings, and after three months, she had completed her contract. She was invited to Washington to be decorated for the work she had done.

At the Pentagon the following day, she heard several times, in casual conversation, of plans for a new preemptive war.

"Would there be a draft?" she asked.

"Probably," they answered.

She drove home subdued and thoughtful. That night she spent two hours in silence by herself. Her 17-year-old son would be eligible for the draft. She pulled out the aquarelle drawings of all the sites she had visited. She selected three abroad, one in Idaho, and the Pentagon itself. She erased them all.

They disappeared. The Pentagon was a gaping hole.

The Military imposed silence on the losses. The media reported losses of life at the bases she had erased, but then fell silent. The rest of the world reacted at first with surprise and then indifference to the disappearance of the bases.

Her thoughts returned to the question of her childhood—where had they gone, and where did they now exist? But now she had an answer. She hadn't seen live people in the shadow-world, but the cat was still alive. Her drawing hadn't included any live people. She had been careful about that. But if people had disappeared with the bases, her consolation was that they would live forever in that other world, "like the cat!" she said. For a moment she was troubled, but then she shrugged.

When the hubbub over the "disappearance" of the defense sites had died down, Max called her.

"You used the aquarelles again, didn't you?"

"Max, I meant to call you, but I was too upset. Yes. I used the aquarelles. In Washington I heard about plans for another preemptive war. No son of mine is going to be drafted for any war."

"But Sacha," Max went on, "people died at those bases when you rubbed them out."

"Maybe," she said. "They disappeared. I'm not sure about *dying*. Remember, the cat was still alive and the dahlia was still fresh."

When she hung up, she sat thinking for a few moments, but then went to bed and fell into untroubled sleep.

She kept her job with the Military. No one seemed to connect her and her drawings with the destruction that went on. She was awed by the power she wielded—a power which the Pentagon would never know, and if they did, they wouldn't believe or understand.

With her daughter, she became a pacifist. Her country began to excel in diplomacy. Each time a move toward war was broached, military bases disappeared.

"It's too bad," Max said to her later, "it's too bad you don't get credit for the long peace!"

"I don't want credit," Sacha said. "The peace is its own reward."

"But Sacha, you deserve the Nobel Peace Prize! Just think . . . .

"Max, don't you think the peace itself is far more important than the prize?"

"Sacha, don't you worry and feel guilty about the people who disappeared when you erased the bases?"

“Friendly fire, Max, friendly fire! Just what they told me when Mike was killed. Unlike Mike, though, they’re still alive, even though it’s just in that Muse-Land.”

“Of course,” Max said. “I agree with everything you’ve done. I just wanted to tease you a little.”

“I can take this consolation,” Sacha responded. “The cat was still mewing; the original dahlia was still fresh. If people passed over into that world when I rubbed out the bases, then they’re still alive. Their problems is that they’re trapped, and they have no way to get back.”

“Let’s leave that, Sacha. What will happen after your death?”

“I don’t know what will happen to the people at the bases I erased, but as for the war problem, that will be someone else’s task. I’m not here to change the world forever.”

“But you have, Sacha. You’ve changed it forever.”

“There could still be wars after I die” she said. “I just hope the diplomats get really skilled at their work and practice diplomacy instead of war.”

“Then live a long life, Sacha, live a real long life.”

THE END

The Stonemason

INTRODUCTION

This is a "What if?" story about Christian belief and teaching. If the power to move people emotionally is considered, the difference between the power of the spoken word and the power of sculpture is sensationalized, perhaps, here.

If the focus is on the written word, then sacred books appear to win; but if the focus can be turned to geography as art, the winner is not so clear. This brief piece examines that difference.

God had an older Son, but no one talks about Him. The younger one got all the attention—a reader, a talker, and a political activist for His Father—or so He claimed. His ideas and communistic love-talk made Him a cultural phenomenon, not His carpentry. It is noteworthy that the symbol with which He is most associated—the cross—wasn't even crafted by Him. So no one can ever know how good He was—as a carpenter, that is.

As usual, it is easy to be sidetracked by Jesus—so attractive! But the older brother merits some attention. He was a stonemason, and He *practised* His craft. He grew up a sort of awkward demiurge dropping things and fumbling things in a way that caused His Father to worry. It was decided that He would be a stoneworker because He was big, burly, and brawny—all those B-words that gave Him His name, Buster.

And how did He learn His trade? With lots of practice! But where was it safe for Him to learn? He was a big boy and a bumbler. So God said to Him, "Go west" and sent Him to the new world where He went wild!

Of course He made mistakes. His biggest and most famous blunder was the Grand Canyon. It was a real eyesore until it weathered a little, and the Colorado River ate into it and carved the bottom. He tossed rocks around and built the Chiricahua hoodoos. He hacked the Mogollon Rim and then tipped it on its side. He did Sedona in His red period, and left His signature all over the landscape. Later, after He had mastered His craft, He chiseled out some small artistic canyons, and then attacked the continent.

God (His Father) shaped the landscape and geography of the Old World—Asia, Africa, Europe. Precision and economy of mountain and river from the neat Nile to the lofty Himalayas are typical. It was North and South America that He left to Buster, and the products of His heavy hand are unmistakable everywhere. Just look at the steep Andes, the vast Amazon valley, and the skinny Isthmus of Panama, or the mess up in the Arctic. And don't forget Alaska—the crown of North America turned sideways. But what could one expect with Buster?

There are samples of His work from the earliest in the rock quarries of Arizona down to the late graceful cluster of Great Lakes and the classically simple bowl of Hudson Bay. Later, when He went interstellar, the work is harder to trace. From the evidence of astronomers, black holes and novas look like signature work—sensational as usual, even when crude.

Buster's work is all visual; His brother's is almost all hearsay oratory. This question arises: Does the visible have more power over humans than the audible? There is no answer to that question, but the question itself confirms the genetic similarity between the two brothers and Their Father: the issue was power over humans. And another question arises: which brother's work will last longer? Will the cultural outlast the geographical, or *vice versa*?

In any case, it seemed important to point out that the much talked-about younger brother did have an older one never talked about. And the work of that older brother bears a lot of looking at and thinking about.

THE END

The Mycenaead: The Trojan War From Mycenae

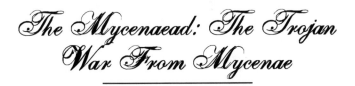

Introduction to The Mycenaead

The Trojan War is a story still taught in courses of myth and legend. Homer, in his Iliad, told that story first. His focus was on the war between Greece and Troy to return Helen to her husband Menelaus. All the kings and princes who had wooed her had sworn an oath to unite for her return if anyone abducted her. Paris, prince of Troy, abducted her; the Trojan War ensued.

The Greeks who listened to Homer knew the background of the whole story. Just as any modern reader in the western world would recognize Biblical references from both the Old and New Testaments, the Greeks knew the gods, demigods, and humans—the heroes and heroines of their complex mythology.

In this retelling of the tale, I have tried to present in speech and story, the background of that epic poem, The Iliad

All of this information will be presented from the viewpoint of Clytemnestra, the wife of Agamemnon the Greek leader in the Trojan war.

THE HOUSE OF TYNDAREUS

Clytemnestra and her older sister Helen loved the stories that their mother, Leda, told them—tales of the gods, of creation, of heroes, and, of course, of heroines. Life in the palace at Sparta moved along like one of their mother's stories until one evening at dinner, when their father, King Tyndareus, argued with some guests about Troy and a shipping-toll. Everyone shouted. She and Helen were frightened and crept to their bedroom.

When Leda came that night to tell them a story, Helen spoke up: "Mother, tell us about Troy and the toll."

Leda pulled up a chair and asked, "Is that what you both want?" When they nodded, she began, "Directly across the sea northeast lies a long narrow channel, the Hellespont, leading from our sea, the Aegean, to the Black Sea, on whose shores fields of grain stretch north and west as far as the eye can sea, like a golden ocean. Troy stands at the entrance to the channel, and every ship sailing up the Hellespont must pay a toll to pass Troy. After you were born, Clytemnestra, your father and I sailed to Troy. Sparta here is poor land for farming, and we need grain from the Black Sea. But to get it, we have to pass Troy. And to pass Troy, we must pay a toll otherwise the Trojans will drop rocks on us from the cliffs above that narrow channel I spoke of—the Hellespont. We disembarked to visit King Priam while the ship sailed up to collect grain. The first thing I noticed was that the Trojans look very different from us. They all have pale eyes and red hair."

"Red like fire?" Clytemnestra blurted out.

"No, not like fire dear—different shades. King Priam and Queen Hecuba both have deep reddish-brown hair. Hector, their heir, is a carrot-top, and Cassandra had gold-pink hair with light blue eyes. Everybody we saw had red hair."

"Tell us more about Troy," Helen directed impatiently. She felt, at 15, some of the responsibility of being oldest child to a king.

Leda leaned back and spoke in the tone she used for mythic tales. "Far away, on a high windy plain overlooking the Aegean Sea, stands Ilium of the topless towers, the city we call Troy. It guards the narrow Hellespont leading north to the fields of grain around the Black Sea. East lies Mount Ida. Southeast stretches a rocky coast. Southwest, across the sea and beyond the islands, run the cliffs of northern Greece. Due west is Mount Olympus, the home of the gods.

"Built on the Scamander River with farmlands around it, the city of Troy is self-sufficient and collects a toll from every ship that sails north to the grain fields. Poseidon, god of the seas, protects it. Since Aeacus founded it and Apollo sang the walls into place, Troy has amassed incredible wealth. So there above the sea, it shines like a city of gold.

"Priam and Hecuba rule there today. When their first son Paris was born, the priests of Poseidon predicted that he would cause the destruction of the city, and advised the king and queen to expose him on Mount Ida. They did it. Their next son, Hector, is their heir. Cassandra, their daughter, is beautiful, looking very much like you, Helen. I met those two. Rumors have spread about all of them and about other children born since I was there. If we can believe the rumors, the god Apollo was so infatuated with Cassandra that he gave her his gift of prophesy. When she chose to become a priestess of Artemis, vowed to chastity, he was enraged. He could not withdraw the gift, but he cursed it so that no one believes her prophecies. Other children are only names to me. But back to Troy. The city is a byword for splendor. People say its streets are paved with gold. With the sea in front and mountains behind, Troy is blessed by the gods."

"Are they much wealthier and more powerful than we are?" Helen asked.

"Oh yes!" Leda counted out their assets on her fingers: "They have farmland to supply their food, a large river of fresh water, a standing army, a warrior king and a warrior prince. Poseidon, brother to Zeus himself, protects them. In addition, they hold the passage to the grain fields around the Black Sea, and the toll they charge keeps their coffers filled with gold. No kingdom can have more wealth and good fortune than they have."

"Don't forget the son with the curse," Clytemnestra murmured.

"I thought you were asleep," Leda said.

"And," Clytemnestra continued in a sleepy voice, "don't forget the prophet-daughter whom no one believes,".

"Yes," laughed Leda, "with all those gifts, there have to be a few curses, and you've named them. Next time," she continued, "I'll tell you about our neighbors at Mycenae."

She blew out the oil lamp, and the two girls lay back for the night.

THE HOUSE OF ATREUS

The next evening, Leda resumed her story. "What I told you about Troy last night is common knowledge. Everyone talks about Troy and its wealth. But what I tell you today is spoken only in whispers."

"Why are you telling us?" Helen asked.

"I'm telling you because this is the world you live in and these are our neighbors in the bay next to us. You are princesses, and the men I talk about tonight are the king and the two princes next door to us. Last night I told you about Troy, a kingdom blessed by the gods. Tonight I'm telling you about Mycenae, a kingdom cursed by the gods.

Leda's voice sank to a whisper. "Mycenae, the city, stands above Port Argos and the great Gulf of Argos north of us. The land is barren, fit only for sheep and goats. More than any other kingdom in Greece, it depends on the grain fields of the Black Sea for food, and so it must have enough money to pay the Trojan toll.

"The last king there, old Pelops, died without saying which of his twin sons was to inherit the crown, so Atreus and Thyestes fought over the kingdom. Your father and I wondered why they fought at all over such useless land. War cost them soldiers and the money needed to buy grain. In the end, Atreus seized the city, and to make peace, he invited Thyestes with his sons to a feast. While the two brothers discussed the division of Mycenae, their children played behind the palace. Atreus's chef captured, killed, and cooked two of Thyestes' sons. He was supposed to kill all three, but the youngest was here with his mother. Atreus served the two children as a stew to Thyestes, with their heads for dessert. At the exact moment when Thyestes recognized his sons, Atreus stabbed him to death.

"He concealed from his own two sons, Agamemnon and Menelaus, what he had done, and set them to work building a fleet of cargo ships to carry grain. Atreus was the brains behind the plan, but his son Agamemnon was the leader. From the age of 15, he sailed the ships up to the Black Sea. Two years ago, when he was 20, he stayed at Troy until the ships returned. King Priam asked Hector to watch him, and of course Hector found him scouting out the defenses of the city. Priam kept him in the palace, and rumor says he saw Cassandra and was smitten. Do you remember her?"

"Yes," said Helen, "she's the prophet no one believes."

"That's right!" said Leda. "Since that visit, Hector and Agamemnon have avoided each other. Unlike Agamemnon, Menelaus, his younger brother, has a pleasing personality. Atreus was careful not to repeat the mistake of his father, Pelops. He named Agamemnon his heir, and then told both boys how he had killed their uncle Thyestes and his sons. He warned them about a third son, but didn't know where he was.

"With their fleet, they have acquired wealth and power by trading. They're successful and resourceful. Atreus has a fleet of ships trading grain, two warrior sons, and an ambition big enough to rule the whole world."

"Where is Thyestes' other son, the child who wasn't killed?" Clytemnestra asked.

Leda hesitated before she answered, "It's Aegisthus at our court. Your father hid him here right under the nose of Atreus." She reached out to hold her two daughters. "But you may never tell anyone what you know—not even Aegisthus."

This story was sobering for both girls. When their mother left, Clytemnestra couldn't sleep thinking of the violence and greed next door to them, for Mycenae lay just around a great headland from Elos, their own port.

HELEN

Two years later, Helen turned 17 and Clytemnestra 15. Visiting princes and kings took one look at Helen, and lingered. She had a blond loveliness that everyone wanted to see, touch, and own. Tyndareus foresaw problems because everyone wanted Helen. Clytemnestra was proud of Helen, and talked with her about how besotted all the men were. Helen seemed annoyed. "They don't love me; they want to own me. They're not interested in me for me; they just don't want anyone else to have me."

Clytemnestra was stunned, but found it true. She told all of this to Leda later, with some wistfulness.

Leda replied coolly, "Helen intoxicates men. Wait until she's married, and the rest will sober up. You're a beauty yourself!"

"But I don't intoxicate men," Clytemnestra mumbled, as she slipped away.

Another two years passed. At 17 Clytemnestra had all the beauty of her mother Leda, but Helen had a radiance that stunned and awed. Kings and princes gathered like moths to a flame. Agamemnon and Menelaus, the princes of Mycenae came to join the other suitors for Helen. Their father Atreus died, and Agamemnon became king of Mycenae, but he stayed in Sparta to vie for Helen.

From the moment she met Menelaus, Helen liked him. Clytemnestra asked, "What is there about him that you like?"

Helen answered, "He's the only one who likes me for myself."

"What do you mean?"

"When I talk to one of the others, they don't even look at me. They look around proudly at all the others as if they've won something. Menelaus is the only one who doesn't show me off when he's with me."

"Why do you think that is?" Clytemnestra asked.

"Because he's a younger brother, and will never be king."

"But Helen," Clytemnestra cut in quickly, "this is your chance to be a queen. He's a younger brother and will never be king. Shouldn't you think about that before you make a choice?"

"No," Helen shook her head, "Menelaus and I would stay here. He doesn't want to live with his brother King Agamemnon, and I'm happy here."

Though baffled by Helen's reasons, Clytemnestra reached over and hugged her. Clytemnestra saw that despite all her beauty and all her suitors, Helen was lonely.

Before Helen chose a husband, Tyndareus planned to demand an oath from all the suitors: they had to swear that if Helen didn't choose them, they would leave peaceably. Leda, Helen, and Clytemnestra had pointed out to Tyndareus how serious Helen's choice would be—broken hearts, hurt pride, and lots of jealousy. Together the four had joked about the oath, and it was Helen who dubbed it "The Great Oath". Before exacting the oath from the suitors, Tyndareus privately consulted the wisest man he knew—Ulysses, king of Ithaca, also one of the suitors. Ulysses suggested that part of the oath should be a promise to unite and bring Helen home if anyone ever abducted her. Hopeful of being chosen, all the suitors took that oath.

When Helen chose Menelaus, Clytemnestra saw relief in both her parents. Most of the suitors left for their homes to seek other wives. Some stayed hoping that Menelaus would die, but after the marriage ceremony, they departed.

After a visit to Mycenae for Menelaus to gather his possession and conclude his business there, the married couple planned to take up residence in Sparta with Tyndareus and Leda. Agamemnon returned to Mycenae with Helen and Menelaus.

A few days after Helen and Menelaus had left for Mycenae, and after all the suitors had departed, Clytemnestra went to her mother's chamber, closed the door, sat down, and began, "I have to talk to you about the triplets. Why are the triplets so different from me and from everybody their age? Six years ago at age 11, Castor and Pollux left to be mercenary soldiers. Helen is two years older than I am, but looks almost as old as you are."

"It's—it's just the way they grew," Leda stammered.

Clytemnestra shook her head and went on, "When I look in the mirror I see your face and your eyes. Castor and Pollux and Helen don't look like you or father. Where did they come from?"

Leda looked frightened, but said, "Why are you asking me?"

"I asked the priests, and they said to ask you," Clytemnestra replied.

"You went to the priests!" Leda gasped, lurching to her feet.

"I asked the priests after the wedding; I was too embarrassed to ask you."

Leda led Clytemnestra to a mirror, and faced her in the glass. Midnight hair, deep blue eyes, and high-cheeked beauty stared back from both faces in the mirror.

"You certainly do look like me! I've dreaded this moment since the three of them were born. I've never talked to your father about them." Leda sat down. "Just before we were married, your father sailed off to visit Atreus, our neighbor next door; I stayed here. The next night, a night of full moon, I walked down to the river. A swan[1] came floating toward me in the moonlight. It was like a dream—what happened then. The swan seized me in his beak, overpowered me with his wings, and—and mated with me. It was bizarre. Your father and I were married two weeks later, and seven months later, I gave birth to two eggs. Your father was away again. From one egg came Castor and Pollux, from the other, Helen. The eggs proved that what I dreamt that night by the river, had happened."

"But the swan!" Clytemnestra exclaimed. "Who was their father?"

Leda's voice shook. "The midwife called the priests. When they found out about the eggs, and saw the three children, they came to me secretly, and told me that the father undoubtedly was—was Zeus!"

"Do you believe it?"

"Look at Castor and Pollux—adult warriors at 11!

"And Helen?"

"Of course—look at her. Your father thinks Helen looks like him. He had light hair as a child, and he loves her. But who could help loving Helen?"

Clytemnestra's sober face changed to a smile. "Yes, who in the world could resist loving Helen?"

Leda hugged her and sighed, "Oh my child, who could resist loving you?"

While Helen and Menelaus were at Mycenae, Agamemnon came back to Sparta to ask for Clytemnestra's hand. She was happy to accept him. Of the two brothers, she preferred Agamemnon who, for all his sternness, seemed more passionate and decisive than Menelaus. Four months after Helen's wedding, Clytemnestra married Agamemnon, sailing down past Elos, and up the Gulf of Argos to Mycenae as Helen and Menelaus returned to Sparta.

Leda had been right. Away from Helen, Clytemnestra was beautiful, like her mother, and in his fierce way, Agamemnon loved her.

Gathering Storm Clouds

Seven years passed. Helen at Sparta had one child, Hermione, who inherited some of her mother's beauty, and all of her father's pleasantness. Clytemnestra at Mycenae had three children. Elektra was like her father, with crinkly hair and a lean athletic body, but she had her mother's deep blue eyes. Orestes, her son, had black hair like his mother and the cool gray eyes of his father. Iphigineia was like her grandfather Tyndareus, a fair child with pale blue eyes, and a radiant smile. She brought joy to them all, softening even the stern heart of Agamemnon.

After the birth of Iphigineia, Leda came from Sparta to visit her daughter. On the first evening, when the children were all in bed, Clytemnestra sat at her mother's feet, and said, "Tell me a story, the way you used to for Helen and me before we got married."

Leda smiled. "Ever since Helen's marriage," she began, "the priests have told me what was going on among the gods. Zeus and Hera hosted a formal banquet for all the gods and goddesses except Eris, the goddess of discord who always makes trouble. Eris was furious, and for revenge inscribed a golden apple, '*For The Fairest Goddess*.' She crept to the door of the banquet hall and rolled the apple into the center. Zeus sent his cupbearer to fetch it, and read out what was written on it, '*For The Fairest Goddess*.' Then he stood frozen in silence. How could he give the apple to one goddess without offending all the others? Aphrodite the goddess of love, Hera the queen of the gods, and Athena the virgin goddess of wisdom, they all stepped forward to claim it. The others watched.

"Zeus asked quickly, 'Who is the handsomest man in the world?' They all shouted, 'Paris on Mount Ida.' Zeus turned to the three goddesses, saying, 'I could not begin to decide among the claims you make. The best judge of who is fairest must be the fairest himself. Paris will make the decision.' He handed the apple to his messenger, Hermes, saying, 'Explain to Paris the honor we have bestowed on him.'

Clytemnestra interrupted her mother. "Is that the Paris who was to be the doom of Troy, the story you told us years ago?"

Leda said, "It must be. I don't understand how it can be, when I know that Priam and Hecuba exposed him on

Mount Ida, but," she murmured, "prophecies do come true, don't they! Anyway, the priests told me that Paris listened to Zeus's message, read the inscription, and looked at the three goddesses. He heard three voices. From Hera, a voice in his ear said, 'If you give me the apple, I'll give you power and wealth.' From Athena, a voice in his head said, 'I'll give you wisdom and everyone will seek your advice.' From Aphrodite, a voice in his heart said, 'I'll give you the most beautiful woman in the world.'

"Stop!" Clytemnestra exclaimed. "I know. He gave it to Aphrodite."

Leda said, "How right you are! Hera and Athena disappeared, Hermes flew back to Olympus, and Aphrodite sat down to instruct Paris. 'First of all, go to Troy. Later, I'll lead you to the most beautiful woman in the world,' and she departed to make a triumphal entry with the apple on Mount Olympus."

"How did the priests know all this?" Clytemnestra asked.

"I don't know, but I believe them."

"And who is the most beautiful woman in the world for this Paris?"

Leda reached out to take both shoulders of her daughter. "I don't want to think of it!" she whispered, "and that's why I told you."

Clytemnestra's eyes slid from her mother's as she whispered back, "It's Helen, isn't it!"

Leda replied, "I'm not sure, but I live in fear. She may, indeed, be the most beautiful woman in the world. I look at her every day, and gasp at her loveliness."

"I haven't seen her since I married—seven years—is she more beautiful now than she was?

"Much more," Leda murmured, "much more. That is what frightens me." Leda sat back and went on, "Paris left

Mount Ida and went to Troy. In Troy, the citizens adored his beauty; Priam saw the resemblance to himself. He's there now, and let's both hope that he stays there."

In the Greek world over those seven years, there had been general discontent. The weather was bad, the harvests were poor, and Greece became more dependent on the grain from the north.

Then Troy raised its toll.

That angered all the Greek rulers. Agamemnon, with his fleet of grain vessels, felt the anger everywhere. He knew that all the rulers, through Helen, were familiar with Sparta, so he suggested that Tyndareus invite the princes and kings of Greece to Sparta for a discussion of the Trojan problem. (Agamemnon had coined that phrase "The Trojan Problem".)

Tyndareus invited Priam, the king of Troy, to come in person, but Priam refused, sending Paris as his representative. Paris, remembering the promise of Aphrodite, was eager to go.

The conference was long and the discussions bitter. The kings who were loudest in their complaints were those who needed grain the most, and hated Troy. The best Paris would offer, speaking for his father King Priam, was to promise that the rate would not rise, but he refused to lower it. The meeting broke up in discontent.

While the meetings and the bickering were going on, Paris and Helen found each other. Did Aphrodite enchant Helen to love Paris? Did Paris win her love? No one knows, but at the end of the conference, Paris left with Helen, who abandoned both Menelaus and their daughter, Hermione. The Trojan ship cast off by night, slipping down the Evrastos River past Elos, the port, before anyone in Sparta could light a beacon to stop them. Then the ship, built for swiftness, not for the transport of grain, sped northeast past the Bay of Argos and across the Aegean Sea to Troy.

Menelaus turned to his father-in-law Tyndareus for advice; he turned to his brother Agamemnon for action. Tyndareus's call went out demanding that all the suitors should fulfill their oaths and come not to Sparta, but to Argos, the port of Mycenae. Golden Helen had been stolen by Paris, prince of Troy.

Agamemnon assumed the leadership of the oath-takers, a leadership to which he felt he was born, and for which he had prayed. Now he had a justification to smash Troy. He could almost taste the fall of the city, and the wealth to come for his fleet. "Helen!" he shouted at Clytemnestra, his cold gray eyes flashing, "Paris! Who cares? They have handed Troy to me!"

When the Trojans looked at Helen and Paris, they forgot the prophesy and loved them. Cassandra prophesied doom, and Laocoon, priest of Poseidon, railed against Paris. In vain! Priam and Hecuba would not listen, bewitched by the beauty of the pair. Hector foresaw what would inevitably happen, for he remembered the prophesy of Paris as Troy's doom, and he knew Agamemnon. And in Mycenae, Clytemnestra, too, knew what would happen for the same reasons.

Weeks passed. Troy continued gathering the tolls, confident that no consequences would follow the abduction of Helen. In prudence, however, they kept their promise: the toll-rate stayed where it was.

THE GREEK DEPARTURE

In Greece, the memory of golden Helen, like an enchantment, drew all the former suitors back to the Peloponnesus to fulfill their oaths. Wives were desolate, and children fretted, but the husbands kept their vows. Hundreds of ships headed for Argos where, over a few weeks, the Gulf filled with them.

The suitors, most now married and eight years wiser, pledged their oaths once more to Menelaus. Agamemnon greeted them with feasting and drinking. Clytemnestra recognized each one of them, and helped Agamemnon host the meetings where they all planned war.

All the suitors with their ships gathered. It would take long to list them all, but a few will give a hint of the strength moored in the harbor. Achilles, who had wooed Helen at age 14, was now a famous warrior at 22, and came with his Myrmidons in twenty ships. Ulysses from Ithaca, the craftiest, brought twelve ships. Idomineos from Crete, the wealthiest, brought one hundred. Agamemnon and Menelaus together furnished one hundred. And so on. But with many ships or few, the wind wafted all the suitors to Argos. They left wives and children at home except for Achilles, who brought his six-year-old son Pyrrhus, already a fierce and argumentative bully like his moody father.

The wind wafted all the suitors into the bay at Argos, but then it fell. In meetings and conferences, all the kings agreed on the destruction of Troy, while they waited for a wind. None came. A week passed. They all saw the hand of heaven, and their seer confirmed it after consulting his oracles.

Calchas, the old gray seer of the Greeks, learned what would bring favorable winds. He waited three days before telling Agamemnon, "Artemis has stopped all the winds because she loves Troy. The only way to raise a wind is to sacrifice your child Iphigineia to Artemis."

Agamemnon told the kings how they could raise the winds. Those with children argued against the sacrifice, those without children shrugged. Agamemnon preempted further discussion: he summoned Clytemnestra with the children to the harbor.

Clytemnestra learned all of this later. At the time, she came obediently with the children. At 27, she could have been her mother Leda. At Argos, as she walked along the pier, with her children, she saw the look in the eyes of all the old suitors. It was the look she had seen as they watched Helen, and she led the children along proudly, conscious now of her own beauty. Elektra at 7 showed a lively spirit like her father. Orestes at 6 was quiet and observant. Three-year-old Iphigeneia had a heart-wrenching blond prettiness. Agamemnon leaned to hug Orestes and Elektra, and reached for Iphigeneia. Clytemnestra gave him the child, and smiled as he lifted her into the air. When he handed the child to Calchas, Clytemnestra clutched at his shoulder in sudden fear.

"What are you doing?" she whispered.

"For a favorable wind, the gods demand her sacrifice," he called out for all his captains to hear.

"No!" Clytemnestra gasped, tearing at his arms.

He shrugged her off and tried to stare her down. Fear and hatred almost stopped her heart. She covered the faces of Orestes and Elektra, watching stony-faced and dry-eyed as Calchas laid the child on the altar, and raised the knife. As the knife came down, Iphigeneia disappeared—Clytemnestra saw this! Agamemnon, grasping her arm and frowning at her, missed the miraculous disappearance of his daughter.

Clytemnestra shook herself free from Agamemnon's clutch, and took the hands of Orestes and Elektra. She looked around at all the suitors as she had done years before in the palace of her father. She recognized them all. The besotted look on their faces brought her no joy. In her mind she screamed "Helen, you did this!" Looking up in despair, she saw flotillas of clouds flying on the wind purchased by her child's death.

She bowed low to Agamemnon, and to all the kings, and with burning eyes, she raised her right hand to point to the sky, "Lord of Mycenae, and all you kings of Greece, former suitors to my sister Helen, see in the sky the clouds flying on the wind that my child's sacrifice has bought for you. May those winds blow you to Troy, and bring to you all, to each of you," here she glared at Agamemnon, "to each one of you, what you deserve. And now, O lord of Mycenae, my husband, may I return to the palace with our—with my remaining children?"

Agamemnon moved to embrace her, but raising both hands, she stepped back, and called out in a voice shaking with rage, "May your enterprise prosper, as it deserves!" Turning, slowly and stately, she led Orestes and Elektra away from the harbor up to the palace at Mycenae.

The suitors murmured together in confusion, and Menelaus turned to question his brother, but Agamemnon called out, "Men of Greece, the wind has come. Let us sail for Troy. Now let this expedition release us from those old oaths. To Troy!" With relief, they all shouted, "To Troy!" and boarded ship.

Though it had taken many weeks for all the ships to gather, it took only half a day for them to disappear from the Gulf of Argos.

HERA'S INTERVENTION

Back at the palace, Clytemnestra found her mother, who had arrived from Sparta. "Where is Iphigineia?" Leda asked.

"Don't ask me!" Clytemnestra shouted as she turned Orestes and Elektra over to their nurse, and climbed to the wall above the gate. Her eyes looked at the ships sailing away, but she saw only Iphigeneia. Out of sight from all, she cried and screamed into the murdering wind. She railed at Helen, but with her blinding tears, she saw! It wasn't Helen! It was the suitors; all of them had left kingdoms, wives, and children for a foolish oath. And above them all, it was Agamemnon. Yes, he had been a suitor too! He had married her, a second choice, and now he had sacrificed her child. To whom? For what? For Helen? No! Clytemnestra knew the answers—for greed and ambition.

Clytemnestra stopped crying. Her breathing returned to normal. Looking up, she cried, "I disown him—he's no longer my husband!" She went down to tell her mother what had happened, adding one detail: "I'm pregnant". Both women wept.

On Olympus, a mighty divinity heard Clytemnestra's scream—Hera, Queen of the Gods. She had always hated the mortal women Zeus seduced, and the children he begat on them. She had hated Leda and her children. But now, watching Leda's anguish and Clytemnestra's grief Hera felt, for the first time, a deep compassion. These two women were victims! Now she hated only her husband's infidelities. In a flash of light she was present to the two women. They fell to their knees before her radiance.

Hera raised them and spoke, "I am Queen of the Gods. I have watched you both. Leda, I watched Zeus betray you, when he left you to explain Castor, Pollux, and Helen to your husband. Clytemnestra, I watched your husband betray you in order to appease Artemis. Gods and men have betrayed you both! I can't undo those betrayals. No god or goddess can sweep back the sands of time. But for both of you, I have a gift."

Clytemnestra spoke, hoarse with rage, "He is not my husband. I disown him."

"And I, Oh Queen of the Gods," said Leda, "felt betrayed years ago, though I had the consolation of three children. But I grieve with my daughter at the treachery of her husband and the heartless demand of Artemis."

"I understand," Hera said. "When I promise you a gift, I warn you that there is no way to undo what has happened. I will give you both the powers of Sight and of Presence. If you gaze into a flame, you may see and hear what lies closest to your hearts. You will be there in person, even if it were across the world from you. And across space, you may talk with each other."

"And may I see Iphigineia?" Clytemnestra whispered. "I saw that she was snatched away before the knife reached her."

"No," Hera answered, "I lack the power to reveal what another god or goddess hides. Your daughter was taken by Artemis. You may not look there. But you may both see the Greeks and the Trojans, and hear what they say."

Clytemnestra laughed mirthlessly. "Good! My revenge may be long in coming, but with this gift, I can anticipate it to the moment."

"Remember, both of you. Gifts are always two-edged; you may see things you want to see, but you may also see things that it were better you didn't see. I give the gift to both of you; it is up to you to judge how to use it." And as she spoke, she vanished.

From that moment, at Mycenae and at Sparta, the two women, in flame or fire, could see and hear what went on afar off, and could speak with each other.

THE VOYAGE TO TROY

With their favorable wind, the Greeks skimmed over the dark blue water toward Troy. No mortal eye had ever seen or would ever see again a fleet like it: one thousand ships sweeping across the Aegean Sea, island to island. The kings were happy to be together again, and Agamemnon, with the expedition afloat, relished every moment that brought him to his great battle.

Those kings with lands along the route hosted the fleet. Fortunately for them, they didn't hear the complaints when they sailed on. The abandoned wives cursed Helen, the oaths, and the oath-takers. If they had not known before that they were their husbands' second choice, now they did. Resentment hung like a black cloud over Greece and all its island kingdoms.

Clytemnestra and Leda heard and felt the anger over all the land. When Leda left to return to Sparta, Clytemnestra remained beyond comfort, but she whispered to her mother, "Iphigineia was alive when Artemis snatched her from the knife."

"Maybe this new baby will replace her," Leda whispered.

"No child can replace her," Clytemnestra whispered moving away.

"But she's not here!" Leda murmured, clutching Clytemnestra again.

Then day by day, in lamp and flame, they watched the Greeks. After a month of sailing, the thousand ships moored in the bay below the Troad, the high windy plain of Troy. Calling the kings to his ship, Agamemnon laid out his plan of attack. He deployed some to the Black Sea to gather grain, some to raid the herds of Troy for horses, and the remainder to beach the ships and build a wall of boats against any attack from the Trojans. They landed unopposed.

Clytemnestra, gazing into a brazier at Mycenae, watched so long that she burned her face and missed the landing. When she could stand the heat again, she watched first the Greeks, and then the Trojans.

The Greeks landed unopposed, but not unobserved. From the high walls of Troy, Priam and Hector looked down, planning for battle and siege. They had a good supply of food, and their water came from a stream which rose in the city. They sent their herds of horses off into the mountains, to stretch out the line of any Greek raid so that the Trojans could break it and kill the horse-thieves. Hector had anticipated this attack from the time he first met Agamemnon years before in Troy. He and his father had prepared for an assault, but Clytemnestra saw their awe at the size of the Greek expedition. They had left out of their plans two factors: Helen with the oaths of the suitors, and the doom laid on Paris by the gods.

Priam called Helen to the wall. It was years since Clytemnestra had seen her and as always, she was stunned by Helen's beauty. Helen pointed out the kings she could remember: Achilles the youngest, Ulysses the cleverest, Idomeneus the wealthiest, Menelaus her husband, and so on. Agamemnon they all knew. When a herald ran toward the city, Hector went himself to find out what he wanted. A parley in a week? Fine.

THE PARLEYS

Every day Hector sent out his light chariots and swift horses to harass the Greeks who had no horses for their war-chariots. He hoped to daunt them with the speed and precision of his cavalry. Clytemnestra, visiting the Greek camp each day, watched their spirits flag.

On the seventh day, the day of the parley, the entire Greek army massed itself in a phalanx below a silent city. Agamemnon, Menelaus, Ulysses, and Achilles approached the Scaean Gate where Priam and Hector stood. Paris and Helen appeared above the gate. A sigh rose from the Greek army—Auburn Paris and golden Helen! Menelaus looked up in hunger, Achilles fidgeted with his sword, and Ulysses gazed in admiration.[1]

Agamemnon didn't look up at all, but kept his eyes on Priam and Hector.

"We are here to do two things," Agamemnon began abruptly, "to bring stolen Helen back to her husband, and to destroy the need for tolls."

"While we might question your choice of words, 'stolen' and 'destroy', still we would concede much to avoid war," Priam replied. "If Helen went back to her husband, and we guaranteed an exemption from tolls, would you return to Greece? Would your oaths be fulfilled?"

"The oaths mean nothing to me," Agamemnon answered at once, ignoring the shock on the faces of Menelaus and Ulysses. "Troy must be destroyed. We won't tolerate a barrier to the grain." Achilles nodded in agreement, looking appraisingly at the city walls.

Priam was surprised, but not Hector, who stepped forward and said, "I have known for years that you were planning this war. Helen is just the excuse. But let me ask you to re-consider. You are far from home, from wives and children, and from your responsibility as kings. Pillagers and pirates are behind you; here you have food problems with no comforts, no firewood, no horses, no women . . ."

"We haven't sailed this far," Agamemnon interrupted, "to be fobbed off with an adulterous woman and a promise. Troy must be destroyed."

"You interrupted me," Hector said quietly, "in addition to the things I mentioned, you lack water. Between our city and the sea, there is no water."

Agamemnon laughed and pointed to the Scamander River. Hector stared at him until the laughter stopped. Then he nodded to the four Greeks, and turned back with his father to Troy.

As soon as Agamemnon had rejoined his army, the Greeks, still in solid phalanx formation, began to march on Troy. Clytemnestra watched in astonishment. So they hoped to take the Trojans by surprise, and conquer the city at once! And there, breaking ranks, running ahead of the army, charged Achilles, the greatest warrior of the Greeks, screaming "Kill! Kill! Kill!" as he jabbed into the air with his right arm, punctuating each word with his sword. As they neared the walls, however, volleys of arrows flew from archers behind the walls onto the Greeks, while the Trojan cavalry, as if materializing from air, attacked on the flanks and behind with more arrows. Decimated by that rain of arrows, the Greek army had to retreat to their boat-wall. Not one Trojan was killed.

When the Greek kings later heard the offer of Priam and Hector, they realized that Agamemnon had abused their old oath and betrayed them. They all wanted to go home.

Clytemnestra almost missed the second parley, it followed so quickly on the first. Next day, Hector sent a messenger to arrange another meeting for that day. Agamemnon, Menelaus, and Ulysses came up from the beach. Hector met them with Paris and Helen.

"You and your Greeks have had a chance to consider what has happened. Now we make the same offer to avoid further shedding of your blood. Will you all return to Greece if we offer exemption from the tolls, and the return of Helen?"

Menelaus raised his hand to take Agamemnon's arm, but Agamemnon shook it off. "No to both offers. Troy must be destroyed."

Helen moved from Paris's side to face Agamemnon. "I told Priam that would be your answer. From the time I met you at my father's court, Agamemnon, I recognized your hunger and your ambition. You're making two mistakes now—a political one affecting these oath-abiding suitors, and a personal one affecting Clytemnestra and your children. Think again!"

"Would you return?" Agamemnon snapped.

"That's not the question," Helen replied. "Hector asked you if you would go back to Greece if I returned and if you were exempted from tolls. That was the question."

Watching, Clytemnestra laughed at Helen's shrewdness, but then gasped. Agamemnon's face darkened. He seized her wrist in one hand, lifting his other arm to strike her. Paris jumped forward between them as Menelaus grabbed Agamemnon's arm. Helen stared unflinching at Agamemnon. "Bully," she said, "I'm not afraid of you."

Agamemnon tightened his grasp, and twisted Helen's wrist. Paris and Menelaus were now locked together like wrestlers.

"Let go of her!" Hector's voice rolled out with a majesty that shook them all. Agamemnon released Helen, and Hector reached forward to draw her behind him. Menelaus and Paris remained locked together until Ulysses hissed into Menelaus's ear, "Stop! This is a parley! You shame us!" Menelaus pushed Paris to the ground and stepped back. Helen raised him.

Looking at the pair, Clytemnestra sobbed. She had never seen such love, nor seen two people so beautiful that they cast a radiance around themselves. At that moment Clytemnestra understood the promise of Aphrodite and the fatal attraction between the two of them.

Agamemnon screamed, "Troy must be destroyed!" and stalked away. Menelaus stumbled after him. Ulysses bowed, saying, "I apologize. We broke the laws of parley."

Hector looked at him coolly, and said, "They will have to sue for any further talks. Parleys are over."

The three turned to Troy. Ulysses caught up with the two brothers as they tore into Agamemnon's tent roaring at each other.

Ulysses turned to the kings as they gathered around, drawn by the noise. "The parley was not a success," he said, "and we should disband until tomorrow. Agamemnon and Menelaus are at odds about how to proceed. Let us leave them for now."

During that night, Troy diverted all the sewage from its latrines and cesspits into the Scamander, and by morning, the Greeks were sick. The smell of vomit, diarrhea, and death hung over the Greek camp like a green cloud. Doubts redoubled in the minds of all the kings, who questioned the oaths, the desertion of their kingdoms and families, the expedition, and their leader.

Even in sickness, though, Agamemnon had charisma and magnetism. He proposed a long-range plan. They would get wood and meat from the small islands off the coast, and slaves and women from the large island of Lesbos to the south. They would dig wells above the tide-line for fresh water. In small expeditions they would burn the villages that provided labor for the city, and they would burn the farms that supplied food. "We'll drive everyone into the city. This is a siege. We'll drive them all inside, and then we'll smash the city. You saw Paris and Helen—she wants to be here! So let's destroy Troy and never pay another toll."

The kings cheered. They had seen Helen with Paris. Now that they had come, they would stay.

And Clytemnestra grudgingly confessed in her heart that for these charismatic qualities she had married Agamemnon.

Two weeks later, Agamemnon requested a meeting with Hector. He pleaded that while most of his troops were ill, the healthy ones were leaving. All the Greek kings agreed, he said, that the expedition had been a mistake.

From her home in Mycenae Clytemnestra gasped, "What a liar!" but Hector could not hear her, and granted three weeks for their departure. To remind them, he sent a small troop each night to shoot fire-tipped arrows into the camp. Each night, the Greeks had to waste water putting them out.

But every day, the Greeks executed their plan for water, food, slaves and women. When their ships left to raid the islands, the Trojans thought they were departing. But Laocoon, priest of Poseidon, warned the Trojans that the Greek ships sailing off by day, returned by night, and that the Greek camp was growing stronger. Now they had horses.

After 2 1/2 weeks, when Hector sent his cavalry to raid the Greeks, some war-chariots rode out against them, and Trojans were killed for the first time. Greek resolve had returned, and they were prepared to stay.

Clytemnestra knew that the long siege would begin, and she could see that Hector and Priam also knew it.

A Change of Heart

Months passed. Clytemnestra delivered a daughter Chrysothemis. She was dark-haired and lean like her sister Elektra. She could never replace Iphigeneia, and accepting that she would never see Iphigineia again, Clytemnestra turned her heart and mind from despair toward vengeance. Simple killing would not suffice. There had to be more! And that "more" came in a flash of insight: Aegisthus! He was the cousin of her husband who had escaped being cooked and fed to his father Thyestes. He was a legitimate heir to Mycenae—a perfect ally.

Through fire she spoke to her mother. "I need Aegisthus here in Mycenae." "Watch out," Leda warned, "he knows the whole story of his father and his claim to the throne of Mycenae. Are you sure that you want him to come to you?"

"Yes," Clytemnestra said. "He can manage the people here who prefer a man to rule them, and together we can plan the destruction of Agamemnon."

"How can you be so sure that Agamemnon will win?" Leda asked.

"Oh mother, Troy will fall. You pointed out that prophecies come true, and Paris stole Helen. That's how it started. Remember, it's Paris who carries the doom of Troy."

"True!. We'll send Aegisthus by ship, but remember that he'll want to kill Orestes too."

"I hadn't thought of that. I'll send Orestes overland to you, and in my letter to Tyndareus, I'll say that your royal court is more suitable for a prince than this war-court that I keep. Let me know when Aegisthus leaves by ship, and I'll send Orestes."

"Clytemnestra, I worry about you."

"Mother, I'm fine. Each day I thank Hera for this miraculous gift."

Aegisthus arrived. More similar to his cousin Agamemnon than to Menelaus, he and Clytemnestra in a short time were lovers, plotting a mutual revenge. After they had been together half a year, some wounded soldiers returned from Troy with news of sickness and stalemate. Then Clytemnestra and Aegisthus began short voyages to visit the abandoned wives in Greece and the Islands.

They agreed that for these trips, Aegisthus would be a nameless ship captain, and each visit would appear to be by Clytemnestra alone. She planned carefully what she wanted to achieve. No splendor. Hair down. No ornaments. Solicitude for everyone. Join them together!

Clytemnestra, having known all of the kings when they were suitors of Helen, could console each queen for the absence of her husband by name. At each visit, Clytemnestra spoke of the dangers they all faced as "deserted wives." She mentioned pirates, pillagers, and invaders. These were a constant threat. She planned with them how they could help and support each other. Beacon fires could pass information from island kingdom to island kingdom.

Toward the conclusion of every visit, she told each queen about the sacrifice of Iphigineia. All of the women were appalled. And each time before leaving, she spoke of her sister Helen: all of the wives, including herself, were second choices; the expedition in expiation of the oath proved it. She turned the oath around: what had bound all of the husbands together, now bound all the wives.

The last visit that she and Aegisthus made was to distant Ithaca, the island-kingdom of Ulysses. Where Helen was a golden flame, Penelope was light and dark, like a cool evening. She was interested in the loose compact of wives, but pointed out that in remote Ithaca, beacons would find little use. Reaching to take her hand, Clytemnestra said, "Send to me. I'll tell the others."

Clytemnestra and Aegisthus discussed how the queens responded to the absence of their spouses. Some ruled in their husbands' name; some took lovers out of fear or loneliness. But whatever they did, they now had each other for support.

The Trojan War

Over the ensuing years, Clytemnestra watched how success favored now the Trojans, now the Greeks. With horses, the Greeks mobilized more chariots, but the Trojans, using fire arrows, confined the Greeks to their camp on the beach at night, and in the dark, they strewed sewage on the plain above the camps, polluting the wells, and causing constant sickness in the invading army.

The one power of Greece that no one could stop was Achilles, their greatest warrior. Wherever he drove in his chariot, with his companion Patroclus and his troop of Myrmidons, the Trojans gave way. But one man couldn't take a city. Over eight years, his scream, "Kill!", and his sword jabbing up in his right hand, daunted the Trojans, but could not win the war.

During one foray into a village near Troy, Achilles captured some priestesses sacrificing to Artemis. He distributed them among the kings, keeping one for himself. That evening, a Trojan herald rode in with the high priest of Apollo, who commanded the release of his daughter, high priestess of Artemis. It was the woman that had fallen to Agamemnon, and fearing the wrath of both Apollo and Artemis, he handed the priestess over to her father. Then he sent a messenger demanding that Achilles give up his woman.

Clytemnestra was amused. "Anyone will do," she whispered scornfully.

In the ensuing argument, the Greek kings were divided. Some supported Agamemnon to whom spoils of war were due; some supported Achilles who had captured the priestesses and shared them; and some supported both of them. The priestess Bryzeis was only a token of the jealousy between the commander-in chief and his greatest warrior. At the meeting next day, they glared at each other. Then Achilles bowed mockingly. "Take her, commander," he said, "enjoy her. But don't expect to see me or my men on the field. Since our attack on the village, since our capture and distribution of the women, we're tired and must rest." He strode off in wrath to sulk in his tent.[2]

Days passed. Achilles' absence gave an advantage to the Trojans. Under Hector, they drove the Greeks back to the boat wall, cleared the entire plain below Troy, poisoned all the wells, and set fire to the boats.

Agamemnon sent for Achilles. No response. He offered to return Bryzeis. No response. As the fires spread, Patroclus quietly donned Achilles' armor without the permission or knowledge of his friend, and led the Myrmidons out to battle the Trojans.

The Trojans fell back, but Hector noticed that this Achilles held his sword in his left hand. Achilles was right-handed. With a small band of cavalry, Hector raced in and slew the armored warrior. The Myrmidons retreated. Stripping off the armor, Hector recognized Patroclus, and left him naked on the field, returning to Troy with Achilles' magic armor.

When Achilles saw the body of his friend, he dashed about howling to take on Troy single-handed and without armor. The kings had to restrain him. He returned grieving to his tent to sulk again.

Clytemnestra watched Achilles' mother, the sea-goddess Thetis, beg new divine armor from the smith-god Hephaestus. Thetis delivered these to her son, reminding him how he could be killed. When he was born, she had held him by his ankle to dip him in the river Styx for invulnerability. That ankle was unprotected. Achilles listened, but didn't hear.

Then with his Myrmidons, Achilles headed for Troy on his chariot next day screaming "Hector! Hector!" Against all advice Hector went out. With his fleet horse, he hoped to out-match Achilles, but Achilles dismounted, and dared him to fight. Hector dismounted. Within minutes of crossing swords, Achilles slew Hector. He slaughtered the horse, and binding Hector to his war-chariot, he dragged his body three times around the silent city, screaming "Hector!" At the Scaean Gate, he hacked and mutilated the body in front of the Trojans gathered on the walls, and dragged it back to his tent.

That night Priam left Troy and rode secretly to the beach. No one challenged his white beard. He slipped into the tent of Achilles and pleaded long and piteously. Achilles would not give up Hector's body, but agreed to show it to Priam. He pulled back the sheet. Hector lay unmarked as in life. Awed by the work of the gods, Achilles yielded the body, and rode as protector with the old king back to Troy.

Next day, Achilles re-joined the daily conference of kings, and told how the gods had healed Hector's body. Clearly the gods favored Troy. Achilles advised packing up and going home. The other kings agreed.

Agamemnon himself was half-persuaded, until Ulysses spoke. "Clearly the gods are divided. Think what it means that Achilles wears divine armor! Balance that with the miracle of Hector's divine restoration! Yes, the gods are divided. So are we. I have a plan to end the war, but no one will listen to me."

Grudgingly, Agamemnon asked for the plan. Ulysses said, "I want to build a huge wooden horse . . ." Agamemnon stopped him, wanting to hear the plan privately first. Ulysses glanced over at Achilles; the two of them understood Agamemnon—he had to be in control.

Clytemnestra in Mycenae knew that too.

Olympus, Mycenae, the Greek Camp, and Troy

Far off on Olympus, Zeus fretted more and more at the steady interference of his gods in the war. Finally he erupted in rage. He reminded them of a prophecy: "Troy shall stand until a descendant of Aeacus, its founder, takes arms against it." He forbade any further intervention. Hera agreed at once; Ares, Apollo, Aphrodite, and Artemis agreed more reluctantly.

Athena had one question: "May we speak to the warriors?"

Zeus conceded, "Words? Yes! Actions? No."

Athena agreed so readily that Zeus wondered what door he had opened to all of them.

In Sparta, Leda had witnessed the order of Zeus. She knew, with deep conviction, what all others seemed to have forgotten: Troy was fated to fall. The gods themselves had foretold that Paris would be its doom. For herself and for Clytemnestra, only one question remained: how would it come about?

During the ten years of Agamemnon's absence, while the wives talked to each other through herald-messengers, and their beacon fires held pillagers and pirates away, Clytemnestra and Aegisthus honed their plan for revenge. Clytemnestra tried to involve Elektra, but Elektra wouldn't believe that her father had killed Iphigineia. In angry retaliation she accused Clytemnestra and Aegisthus of being lovers. Clytemnestra agreed; it was true. She acknowledged that they had become lovers soon after Aegisthus had arrived, and she smiled to herself knowing she was loved by both the legitimate kings of Mycenae.

Aegisthus and Clytemnestra forced Elektra to marry a farmer. The degradation pleased Aegisthus for what Atreus had done, and eased Clytemnestra's anger toward Elektra. She and Aegisthus were happy together, knowing they had the support of the other queens of Greece and the Islands.

During the construction of the wooden horse, Leda watched Athena prophesy to Ulysses in a dream. "Troy can be destroyed only if a descendant of Aeacus, its founder, fights against it. Pyrrhus, the son of Achilles, is descended from Aeacus through his mother. If Pyrrhus fights against Troy, it will fall." Then she faded.

Pyrrhus was overjoyed. A bloodthirsty bully like his father, he welcomed the prospect of battle at age 16.

The Greeks placed Pyrrhus with a few of their best warriors in the horse. They left a Greek spy to feign illness and talk with the Trojans. Then, they launched their fleet, and sailed out of sight from Troy.

The Trojans rode out to the Greek camp. They saw the giant horse, and they found a sick Greek who revealed that the horse, sacred to Poseidon, had been built as an offering so that the fleet could sail home in safety. He said, furthermore, that it had been built too big to pass through Troy's gates, because the horse brought with it the blessing and help of the god.

As the story spread through Troy, Laocoon, the priest of Poseidon, shouted, "The god would never return to us through a wooden horse!" But when two serpents from the sea killed him and his two sons, the Trojans were convinced that their priest had been punished for doubting. To regain the protection of Poseidon, they dragged the horse to the walls, smashed a gate, and hauled it triumphantly into the city.

Clytemnestra shouted to Leda, "How can they be fooled so easily?" Leda responded much more fatalistically, "Troy is doomed. It was foretold, as you reminded me. We're just witnesses to how the prophesy is being fulfilled."

The fleet was gone, the sea was clear, and the horse was in the city. For the first time in ten years, the Trojans slept free from fear and worries.

The Sack of Troy and After

The Greek fleet returned in darkness. At midnight, the warriors in the horse threw open the gates of the city, and Agamemnon's army came with fire and pillage, to overrun Troy in two hours. Paris slew Achilles with an arrow through his ankle. Pyrrhus butchered Paris and then Priam. Menelaus rushed about looking for Helen. When he found her, he lowered his sword, and said simply, "Come home!" Clytemnestra and Leda watched it all in wonder.

Agamemnon, remembering his visit to Troy years before, went to the temple of Artemis and took Casssandra as his slave. He destroyed the toll-ships, and threw down what was left of the city. Now he was the master trader of Greece with grain ships to transport the wheat from the Black Sea. He didn't need a Troy!

With the fall of Troy and the return of Helen to Menelaus, all oaths were fulfilled. Now Greece had free access to the grain on the Black Sea. Agamemnon left triumphant, with his booty, Cassandra, beloved of Apollo. As he sailed down the

Aegean Sea, the beacons told Clytemnestra that a victorious Agamemnon was on his way home. She had known before anyone, but she thanked her informants through the beacons.

Clytemnestra and Aegisthus prepared Mycenae for Agamemnon's arrival. Workers cleaned the palace and scrubbed the entrance steps. Clytemnestra's maids brought from their chapel the holy crimson veils, sacred to the gods. She dressed herself in black and white, with silver bracelets, a silver necklace, and a silver headband holding back the masses of her black hair. Eyes glittering with triumph, she watched his ship sail into the Bay of Argos, and waited behind the great door at the palace for his arrival. Two chariots drove up to the entrance. In the first stood Agamemnon alone; in the second, stood Cassandra, tied with golden cords.

Before the chariots had stopped, Clytemnestra swept out from the doorway and advanced to the first one, blocking Agamemnon's descent with a profound bow. From the ground she began: "Hail lord of Mycenae, hail commander of Greece, hail conqueror of Troy! Welcome to your kingdom, and to your home. For ten years, we have missed you and yearned for your return. Our watches have been long and tearful, our supplications and sacrificed to the gods constant, with one plea only: send Agamemnon once again to Mycenae."

From his chariot Agamemnon looked with admiration and wonder at this woman, his wife. In her dark glory she was a worthy child of Leda. She continued, "For you and for your return I have commanded my maidens to bring the scarlet tapestries sacred to the gods from the temple, so that they may be spread under your feet as a symbol of the glory and triumph in which you come."

She waved and the maids came forward to spread the temple draperies as a scarlet carpet from the chariot to the door of the palace.

"Daughter of Leda," Agamemnon said, "it would be presumptuous of me to walk on those sacred tapestries. I cannot be so bold."

"Husband, and father of my children," Clytemnestra spread wide her arms, "where in Greece is there anyone of such worthiness to tread on the cloths of the gods who, themselves, stood by you in the long siege? Would Priam himself not walk on them were he the victor? Did the gods not counsel you how Troy might be brought down? It is entirely appropriate that their crimson veils should lead you into your palace."

"Daughter of Leda, I must still decline so rash an act. Let me set foot on the bare earth, and let us enter the palace together. And let care be given to this daughter of Priam, Cassandra, who is one of my spoils of war."

"My king, your word is my law." Clytemnestra rose to her feet, clapped her hands and directed her handmaids to untie Cassandra. Knowing that she still held his rapt attention, she turned again to Agamemnon, "O son of Atreus, you see before you the daughter of Leda and of king Tyndareus of Sparta, my home kingdom, where even now my father entertains your younger brother with his wanton wife, my older sister Helen. Who worthier than you to walk on these tapestries? Don't hesitate. Come, enter your palace. The bath is prepared where you may cleanse yourself and wash away the weariness of your long travels. And then let us take thought on Sparta."

At Clytemnestra's sly declaration of Agamemnon's claim, through her, to the throne of Sparta, his eyes gleamed with greed. Unthinkingly, he descended and trod the blood-red carpet alone, ahead of his wife, into the palace. Avoiding the carpet, she followed.

As they disappeared inside, Cassandra shouted to the people there, "Why don't you follow them inside? Don't you know what that woman and the son of Thyestes will do to your king? How can you stand outside here gazing at me, when murder is prepared within?" Turning to Elektra, she said, "Daughter of Agamemnon, don't you know the revenge that your mother has planned for the man who sacrificed her daughter Iphigineia? Go in! Stop them!"

The curse of Apollo prevented Elektra from believing the prophesies that Cassandra uttered. But what they all could believe moments later was the noise from within: screams "Iphigineia! For Iphigineia!"—shouts "Now, son of Atreus, this is how your cousin avenges his father and brothers." And as a background to all these screams and shouts, came the steady roar of Agamemnon "Murder, murder!" as he was killed.

Clytemnestra staggered out, her arms covered with blood, holding a two-headed axe. "He is dead. Agamemnon, the murderer of Iphigineia, is dead," she said. "Now Aegisthus, the rightful king of Mycenae, will rule."

The servants fled. Mother and daughter glared at each other.

"Now do you believe that he killed your sister?"

"No," Elektra said, "you only killed him for Aegisthus."

"Wrong! But you can't stay here, nor can Cassandra." Walking over, she struck Cassandra with the axe. "The same weapon has killed the two of them."

"Beware, mother!" Elektra cried. "The same fate may befall you and Aegisthus. Remember, Orestes must be reckoned with! Will he believe your tale of Iphigineia and accept Aegisthus?"

Clytemnestra lunged toward Elektra, but she fled.

The Coming Of Orestes

From her palace spies Clytemnestra learned that Elektra inspected each arrival at the harbor, looking for Orestes. Elektra was looking for a second Agamemnon, but Orestes resembled Clytemnestra, with dark hair and a sculpted face. It was he who recognized her. They met secretly, fearing Aegisthus. At first Orestes had no heart to kill either his mother or Aegisthus, but with Elektra driving him on, he agreed to kill both.

When he walked into the palace, Clytemnestra recognized him. "So, you've come at last. Your father had to die. He killed Iphigineia for a wind to waft him to Troy. If you must kill me, do it now. I die happy in my revenge!"

She watched her son, the image of herself, with his father's gray eyes, walking toward her with his sword drawn. She saw the sad look on his face, but a determination like that of Agamemnon when he sacrificed Iphigineia. She screamed at the memory, and shouted to Orestes, "Remember, Aegisthus is your cousin, the son of Thyestes whom your grandfather Atreus killed. He will kill you." At the first blow from the sword, Clytemnestra shrieked and heard an echoing scream from Elektra, a scream of triumph, and a long wail from Leda, her mother, bursting through the door, too late to save her.

The End

FOOTNOTES:

1 ***Leda and the Swan***

And how can body, laid in that white rush,
But feel the strange heart beating where it lies?

A shudder in the loins engenders there
The broken wall, the burning roof and tower,
And Agamemnon dead.
[William Butler Yeats (1923)]

2 Was this the face that launched a thousand ships
And burned the topless towers of Ilium? . . .
Marlowe-Doctor Faustus

3 Homer's Iliad starts at this point: "Sing, Goddess, the wrath of Achilles"

Pronunciation of Greek Names

The accent in almost all Greek proper names comes on the second-last syllable

Agamemnon	a-ga-MEM-non
Achilles	a-KILL-eez
Aphrodite	a-fro-DIGHT-ee
Argos	ARE-gos
Athena	a-THEE-nuh (TH as in theatre)
Bryzeis	bree-ZAY-is
Clytemnestra	clight-em-NES-truh
Electra	ee-LECK-truh
Elos	EE-loss
Evrastos	ee-VRAS-toss
Hector	HECK-tor
Hera	HERE-uh
Hermes	HUR-meez
Idomineos	ee-**do**-mi-NAY-us (a little accent on "**do**")
Ilium	ILL-ee-um (accent on first syllable)
Iphigineia	**if**-i-jin-NAY-uh (a little accent on "**if**")
Leda	LEE-duh
Menelaus	me-ne-LAY-us
Mycenae	my-SEEN-ee
Olympus	owe-LIM-pus
Orestes	owe-RES-teez

Pyrrhus	PEER-us
Scaean	SKEE-un
Scamander	ska-MAN-dur
Sparta	SPAR-ta
Troy	TROY
Tyndareus	**tin**-duh-RAY-us (a little pat on the first syllable "**tin**")
Ulysses	you-LISS-eez
Zeus	ZUSE

Solomon Bar-Levin

Introduction to Solomon Bar-Levin

Anyone thinking about Bar-Abbas may wonder how he explained to himself his last-minute reprieve from death row. Here is one answer. The story's development is unusual, and is completely a creation of imagination. The notes at the end, however, present materials which perplex students of the New Testament to this day.

I

At first there was only relief—he wasn't going to be crucified! The crowd had shouted his name—*his* name—to be freed. Then there was curiosity: who had been chosen to die in his place? Then there was vindictiveness: Bar-Abbas wasn't his real name—his family would know he had been spared, and would live in fear of his reappearance. Let them worry! He would deal with them later.

Between the opening of his cell door and the dazzling sunlit plaza, he became faceless and nondescript—an invisible pickpocket. That was how he had begun his life of crime. No one in the plaza recognized him. In his dun clothing, he faded through the crowd as he had learned to do. Over there was the man—the man that the crowd had chosen to die in his place.

"What did he do?" he asked a Roman guard linked arm-to-arm with his fellows to hold back the crowd.

"He preached love and spoke against the religious leaders."

"That's just talk-talk-talk! What did he do?"

"That's all—talk-talk-talk—except once in the temple. He messed up the money-lenders. That's what we heard. We aren't allowed to go in there."

Bar-Abbas turned away impatiently, and followed the crowd. He watched and listened through the hours until the man they called "Prophet" had died. No fighting. No cursing. Only mealy-mouthed forgiveness!

And yet, he thought, what a revenge! To forgive the killers! That left the forgiver in charge and command—the tables neatly turned!

He drank no wine that day, and slept with the animals in a stable for warmth. Should he go home? Should he resume his name, Solomon Bar-Levin? His father had disowned him when he first went to prison. How would his father treat him now? Solomon had the answer at once: his father would treat him as his father had treated him all his life—with indifference.

He had been in conflict with his family since he could remember. His brother Daniel, eight years his senior, was the favorite. Solomon always had felt like a nuisance to his mother and father. From his first word, "Why? he had been contrary and a problem from then on. He was clever, but he had a smart mouth and no respect for anyone or anything.

In Cilicia he grew up speaking both Hebrew and Latin, for although they were Jews, they were Roman citizens. His father Levin Bar-Laban was a prosperous Pharisee and a teacher—too busy to pay much attention to his second son. When Solomon turned seven he began Torah study. As it turned out, Solomon had the brains; Daniel had the looks and the personality. His father noticed the brains. When Solomon turned ten, his father hired a Greek tutor for him—for him, not for Daniel! Levin evidently saw that Solomon was a born scholar, and could be a great academic, but he said nothing to the boy.

His contrariness was not resolved by education. It seemed as though the more he learned, the greater a problem he became to his family both in word and in deed.

Solomon quickly mastered the language and then the subjects in Greek—physics and mathematics. His prime interest, though, was in Greek language and thought. He encountered Socrates (through Plato)—the Socrates who asked questions and more questions. Often the questions were without answers. Often questions were answered by other questions. And occasionally a question was answered by a myth—a story or parable. The writing of Aristotle, on the other hand, reminded Solomon of Torah teaching—answers and more answers. He liked that too, but it was an intellectual dead end.

In adolescence he became unmanageable at home. He loved learning, and he loved his tutors, but he could not tolerate discipline from his family. When he wanted more expensive scrolls to study Greek more deeply, he became a pickpocket, and studied the scrolls in his bedroom.

"Where did you get the money for those?" Daniel asked, pointing to the new scrolls.

"I asked mother," Solomon answered, but the lie was so patent that Daniel and his mother reported it to Levin Bar-Laban. Solomon never forgot the beating from his father that followed.

The next month, when he turned 16, the family moved to Jerusalem where his father became a teacher at the Great Temple. By then Solomon spoke Hebrew, Latin, and Greek. He abandoned his life of petty crime. Studying Torah at the Temple under the great Gamaliel, he proved to be an excellent student. There wasn't a phrase in the legalistic parts of Exodus, Leviticus, Numbers, and Deuteronomy that he didn't know. It was like Aristotle—answers-answers-answers.

In Jerusalem, he found women. He knew sex; women were new! Apart from studying, he was out trying to satisfy an appetite that was insatiable. If his family was aware, they said nothing. Winks with leers from Daniel implied accusations, but Solomon pretended not to see. His father ignored him as usual.

When Solomon was 19, his father was appointed a chief teacher in Jerusalem, and became more pious, more observant, more demanding of his wife and children. Daniel, now 27 and unmarried, pleased without effort; Solomon lived with constant reprimands. All day he heard, "Honor your father."

Then Solomon's knowledge of Torah paid off for him. Criticism in the house reversed. He confronted his father and mother with every failure to observe obscurities of the laws in the Torah—and outside the Torah. Solomon made up laws:

"Speak unto the children of Israel and say unto them . . . ." When his father discovered the mis-statements, he slapped Solomon around for being impious.

He abandoned Torah study and took up his life of crime again. He stayed out at night stealing in the streets. In time he found the streets and market place dangerous with eyes everywhere. So he moved his theft to inns and caravan hotels—the caravanserai—which were safer to rob. And women became an obsession.

When he stayed out overnight, his father confronted him. "What are you doing? Where do you go?" his father barked.

Solomon shrugged. Silent rage flowed like a hot river around the whole family, and Solomon continued his life of crime.

Then he brought a Roman girl into the house through his bedroom window. Their noise brought the family into the room. The arrogance of the girl was beyond measure. Claiming Roman citizenship, she faced down Solomon's father, and walked boldly out, remarking insolently to his mother, "He's quite a son."

The slapping and beating that followed covered his body with bruises and his face with scratches and fingernail gouges that marked him for life.

"Now they won't find you so attractive," Daniel sneered.

A few days later, he found Daniel in his room, inspecting new scrolls and a pile of stolen goods. Daniel whispered, "You'll end up in prison!" Solomon took Daniel's arm and escorted him out the door. Almost immediately, a small troop of Roman soldiers arrived at the house. Solomon threw all the stolen material that he could out his window, but there was enough left in the room to assure his conviction as a thief.

"Come back when you're over it," his mother whispered as he was led out.

His father glared; Daniel smirked.

The charge was petty theft; the punishment—a public whipping. The family was humiliated and Solomon Bar-Levin became a name of guilt and scorn.

Afterwards, knowing the shame he had brought to his family, he did not go near them. He slept in the stables at a caravanserai, and lived on scraps. The scars from his whip-weals branded him for life. He begged in the marketplace, and never acknowledged people who recognized him. For three years he existed like that. By now he was 23.

When he had enough money, he joined a caravan traveling to Egypt. On the fourth night out he was found picking his way through a purse. In the fight that followed, Solomon knifed the owner of the purse, but was overpowered by other travelers, and tied up by the caravan security guards. Almost all of the booty that fellow-travelers had complained about was found in Solomon's bag.

For theft he might have been condemned to prison, but the man whom he had stabbed died, and Solomon knew that he would be executed.

As a Roman citizen he demanded Roman law. With that claim, his family learned of his criminal life. Since there was no Roman Governor at the time in Jerusalem, he had to remain in prison until one was appointed. His family visited. In the visitors' room, the family of four stared at each other like strangers.

His mother started, "How could you . . ." His father interrupted, taking his wife's arm, and saying, "Be silent!"

Levin glared at his son and said, "You will not shame me or this family any longer, Solomon. I disown you!"

Solomon stared, wondering whether he should claim that they bore some responsibility for the bad choices he had made, but in all honesty, he couldn't blame anyone but himself. He stepped back from them and spoke clearly, "I won't shame you any longer. I'm changing my name to Sol Bar-Abbas—Sol son-of-the-father—a new father I now have to replace the one I never had!"

Without another word the family left. His father led the way, holding his wife's arm firmly. His father announced publicly his act of disowning Solomon, and published his new name—Sol Bar-Abbas. Those who knew the family approved of the action, and the new name, Bar-Abbas, was recognized everywhere in Jerusalem: Bar-Abbas—thief and murderer.

It was two years before a new Roman Governor was appointed to Jerusalem.

Facing the Governor, Solomon pleaded self-defense. The Governor watched, and listened, and without a word condemned him to death by crucifixion the week following the Jewish Passover. As Bar-Abbas he became famous: a Jew, and a Roman, condemned under Roman law to crucifixion. His family never appeared, but Sol kept track of them and knew that they were aware of his impending death.

And now at 26 he was free—from both prison and sentence of death. For safety he changed his name from Sol Bar-Abbas to Saul of Cilicia. He had the accent of that northern province, so he took the place-name. He moved about for a few days living once again in stables, and when he felt equal to the confrontation, he went home.

His father answered the door when he knocked, and drew back sharply from the stable smell. Saul stared at him saying nothing.

"Who are you, and what do you want?" Levin began.

"What kind of welcome is this?" Saul mocked. "Don't you recognize the scars, father?" he jibed, pointing to the old fingernail scrapes on his forehead. His mother and brother appeared behind his father.

"Why didn't they execute you like other murderers?" his brother spat.

"Oh! You!" his father said bitterly. "Why did you come back?"

"Why did I come back?" Saul began, still mocking. Inside himself a fierce inquiry began. Why did I come back? He heard again the forgiveness called from the cross. In his head he re-worded his father's question: "Why was I sent back?" His eyes turned from his family, and he said aloud, "Why was I sent back?"

He turned and stumbled through the door. That question was screaming in his head, over and over again, "Why was I sent back?"

II

Drinking—visiting old haunts—encountering old acquaintances—nothing could stop that burning question, "Why was I sent back?" Each place he visited, each person he met, each thing he did—each one whispered the same bleak answer: "You weren't sent back for this!"

Around Jerusalem he heard about the followers of the new Prophet. For a month he wandered around listening to the rumors: risen from the dead! then ascended into heaven! About a week later he was sobering up one morning when he saw a crowd and heard the Prophet's followers talking in tongues. Their leader was Simon Bar-Jonah, renamed Peter. In the afternoon, now cold sober, he knew that the answer to his question was connected to the prisoner for whose death his own life had been exchanged.

Still wandering homeless, he saw a man called Stephen, a follower of that new Prophet, stoned publicly for blasphemy. Then, little by little, piece by piece, he gathered information about the man. His teachings, supposedly against the law, were more like a re-interpretation of the law. Through anecdote and conversation he learned about the preaching.

Saul liked that kingdom "not of this world", and many of the parables. "It's like Plato," he muttered to himself. The social teaching was something different. He was sure that it derived from desert society and desert living—share all to survive. But the love-stuff troubled him. He had been a criminal too long to believe that enemies would—or could—forgive and love. Not even families could do that!

However, he found himself interested and absorbed. He took a job riding security for caravans. Having robbed them in his youth, he was skilled at his job and could spot potential ambushes from miles away. He knew the desert routes, and bandit tactics from first hand. He was first choice for the "long-fars"—the caravans that made long journeys to distant destinations.

Riding security was boring, and left Saul time to think and to meditate. More and more frequently he puzzled over the questions "Why was I sent back?"

Oftener and oftener in Jerusalem he heard stories of the Prophet. Saul liked the way he had avoided saying, "I don't know" and gave a parable. Saul found it Platonic—much like what Socrates would have done with one great difference—Plato's questions were philosophical; this man's questions were social and religious. All the parables and teachings seemed to hang around the three big questions: Where do I come from?, Why am I here?, and Where am I going?

In Jerusalem he studied Torah again between caravan trips. He was dissatisfied all over again as he had been in his adolescence. It was all the same—commandments without reasons, rules and precepts without a purpose. It was like Genesis: "Don't do it—shut up! Just don't do it!"

These problems festered in his mind, his soul, and his heart. When he saw his family, he turned away. He was nameless, a stranger in his own city. More and more he rode caravan security to brood over his question, trying to arrive at some kind of answer.

When he was 43, he took a job with a large caravan from Jerusalem to Damascus. Most robberies took place within riding distance of a city, so for the first two nights he had little sleep.

Then early on the third day he was seared by a blinding light, and snatched up bodily from his horse into the sky. He hung between heaven and earth, feeling naked and unprotected. A voice shouted at him, "Saul, Saul, why do you avoid and persecute me?" He was cast to earth unconscious. He woke up in the security wagon, and when he opened his eyes, he was blind. He staggered and blundered his way around the wagon until his fellow-security guards pushed him to a seat out of sight from the caravan leaders.

"I'm blind. I'm blind," he kept murmuring. When he fell silent, the others questioned him in agitated whispers. "What happened to you? We thought you were dead. Do you have the falling sickness?"

"What happened?" he asked.

"You stood up on your horse and shouted some words, and then tumbled off. We couldn't make any sense out of you, and brought you here to the wagon. Your mind had gone away. When did you come back? What brought you back?"

"I don't know; I'm blind. I can't see anything. How can I work?"

"Don't worry," the chief of security said, "Rest now and we'll see what to do about your sight in Damascus. We don't want to lose you."

Saul returned to his pallet. He had lots of questions: where had he gone? who had shouted at him? why was he blind? why was he sent back? "I'm always being sent back," he muttered.

His sleep was troubled as he tried to find answers. One thing became clear: the voice asking, "Why do you avoid and persecute me?" had to be the new prophet. No one else troubled him as much as that man who had died in his place.

For the rest of the trip to Damascus he was broody and withdrawn. In Damascus, after visits to many healers, he was still blind. Then out of nowhere, a man called Ananias cured him of his blindness by simply invoking the name of the new Prophet. Never had the sun shone so bright nor had colors been so vivid! That raised a big problem for Saul: was that new Prophet what his followers called him—the son of God? On the way to Jerusalem, he decided to find out more about the man, more about his teachings, and certainly more about his death.

III

Back in Jerusalem he cut his hair and shaved his jutting beard—a beard which had expressed his aggressiveness since adolescence. And he changed his name again—not back to Solomon Bar-Levin, nor back to Sol Bar-Abbas, but from Saul of Cilicia to Paul of Tarsus. None of his old acquaintances recognized him; his father and brother passed him on the street without a glance.

Now he walked boldly among the Apostles of Jesus, studying them, and listening carefully to what they said.

Peter was the simplest and the most direct. They said he had been a fisherman. He acted like one. He could add you up—and subtract you—with one glance of those flashing dark eyes. Talking, Peter cut things to the basic issues; he clearly had no time for fluff. His brother Andrew was sharper and talked even less.

Paul had encountered doubting Thomases in the Platonic dialogues. And the Prophet echoed Plato with his statement, "Blessed are those who had not seen and have believed." James was a lightweight, Paul decided, though he admitted to himself that what James said arose from soul-searing experience. In Paul's view, Simon the Zealot had taken all the rabid nationalism that drove him and transferred it to the love message and the social philosophy of the Prophet, but the fierce zeal he brought to this new view frightened his listeners and almost undid the content of the message. Finally, Paul could sympathize with Judas Iscariot, the other zealot, who had hoped that this Prophet would be King of the Jews, and felt betrayed at the triviality and earthly impotence of the kingdom that Jesus preached.

Though Mark was not one of the twelve Apostles, Paul found in him an untutored scholar. Everything he said was in sequential order, and Paul admired his directness. Of the other six, Paul was impressed by only two: James and John.

James was a rough-tough older brother, fiercely proud of the younger one he had protected. But John! John had the face and the eyes. He was soft-spoken and held your attention without trying. Almost all of his talk and his remembrances were about the soft, the gentle side of the Prophet-Teacher.

John was all about love and full of poetic non-answers, and he was unforgettable.

John's story of the bread and wine fascinated Paul:

> *I am the living bread which came down from heaven: if any man eat of this bread, he shall live for ever: and the bread that I will give is my flesh, which I will give for the life of the world.*
>
> *Verily, verily, I say unto you, except ye eat the flesh of the Son of man, and drink his blood, ye have no life in you.*
>
> *Whoso eateth my flesh, and drinketh my blood, hath eternal life; and I will raise him up at the last day.*
>
> *For my flesh is meat indeed, and my blood is drink indeed. He that eateth my flesh, and drinketh my blood, dwelleth in me, and I in him.*
>
> *He that eateth of this bread and drinketh of this wine shall live for ever.*
>
> (*John 6:51,53-56,58*)

Paul asked, "Did he really state, 'eat my flesh and drink my blood'?"

They answered as with one voice, "Exactly as John says."

Paul walked away. It was outside the Torah and the Law. It was Mithras—the Mithraism of the Roman army, where the sanctified priest, clothed in the two-pronged hat, the epauletted vest, and the scarlet cloak, slew the god-as-bull, the bull-as-god, and distributed its flesh and blood to the believers. The new prophet took the Mithraic sacrament under the guise of a vegetation god where the grain was body and the wine was blood.

Paul felt for a certainty that it was Mithras re-worked. He puzzled over it until he had given it a meaning. This food was a shadow, a reflection of sustenance from another world. Bread and wine, through a verbal ritual, became the body and blood of the god. It was Plato as well as Mithras. It was one of his favorite myths—the cave myth. Of course, strength had to come from bread and wine, but they were the shadows of food from an ideal world of forms.

In the *Allegory of the Cave*, Plato presented his belief that the world of sensation was not the real world. Things seen, sensed, and touched were only shadows cast on a cave's blank wall from which humans couldn't turn away. The shadows were cast from a world of primordial forms—ideas—and everything in the sense-world was a shadow of the original Idea in that *real* world, ideas which could only be apprehended intellectually. That myth contained all truth as Paul understood it, and he held it as a touchstone for everything that he studied. He cast the teachings of this new Prophet in the clothing of that myth.

Paul had his insight and his answer. Emboldened by what he considered to be a deeper knowledge, Paul came back to the twelve. Many of them were fishermen. What had a carpenter to do with fisher-folk? Most of them were more non-descript; many of them were of a class that Paul's father would have decried and despised, but Paul knew that in this situation, his father was wrong. The Prophet had *chosen* these people, and Paul had to accept that choice. But beyond that and for a certainty, they had all experienced something profound. They were all convinced, and they all agreed.

He became a listener. And then he became a believer. He absorbed the teaching like a sponge. Paul could speak and preach fluently, passionately, and charismatically. His was the voice of authority. He was aware that he filtered all the prophet's teaching through a Platonic prism, but Paul was convinced: "If he had known, he would have said what

I say . . ." was transformed with time to "He must have meant . . ." In addition, Paul was an expert in Torah and knew the law. He had, after all, been a disciple of the great teacher Gamaliel!

After a year he asked if he might carry the prophet's message abroad. All the Apostles were pleased by the request. This was a man who could move people with the message, and in addition to all his qualifications as a Jewish scholar, he spoke Greek.

Before he left on his ministry, Paul sought out his family. Could the wounds in the family relationships be healed?

They didn't recognize him. Now they could no longer look down on him. He spoke with a voice of authority, and his presence filled them with an uncomfortable awe. When he confessed that he has become a believer in the new Prophet, his father tore the blasphemy seams of his garments.

Paul laughed. "You condemned me for being a criminal believer, and now you condemn me for being a virtuous non-believer. Is your way the only way? Do you have all the answers? Or do you remember the questions? Whatever you say doesn't matter. I'm going away, and I don't know when I'll be back."

They parted in silence and bitterness. Paul experienced a deep sadness; his family felt only bitterness.

IV

Before starting on his mission, Paul prayed with a fervor and zeal he had never experienced before. His plan was simple: teach the message from Antioch through Cyprus,

Asia Minor, and Anatolia. Then return to Antioch. Those were the practical aspects of his planned trip. The ministry aspects were harder to deal with but he set his well-trained and disciplined mind to the task.

That first missionary journey lasted many years and was a resounding success for Paul. His passion and charisma converted hundreds and thousands of followers. These were the Gentiles to whom he felt the message of the new Prophet was intended. On his return to Antioch, he heard of some back-sliding among his converts, and he penned one letter first to the Thessalonians, and one to the Galatians. They were letters of such power that copies spread among the followers everywhere.

He returned from Antioch to Jerusalem, and there had his first discussion—confrontation—with Peter. It ended in agreement, and he prepared for his second longer journey.

From Jerusalem he traveled to Corinth where he stayed for almost a year. Then he went on to Ephesus, Macedonia, Illyria. He returned to Corinth again, and finally traveled back to Jerusalem. As he moved he kept track of the growth and development of his believers in the places he had visited. To the Corinthians he sent a letter that echoed around the world. He didn't use the word "love" which he knew from his early life meant different things to different people. He used the word "charity" instead.

This passage moved all who heard it or read it.

> *Though I speak with the tongues of men and of angels, and have not charity, I am become as sounding brass, or a tinkling cymbal. And though I have the gift of prophecy, and understand all mysteries, and all knowledge; and though I have all faith, so that I could remove mountains, and have not charity, I am nothing.*

And though I bestow all my goods to feed the poor, and though I give my body to be burned, and have not charity, it profiteth me nothing.

Charity suffereth long, and is kind; charity envieth not; charity vaunteth not itself, is not puffed up, Doth not behave itself unseemly, seeketh not her own, is not easily provoked, thinketh no evil; Rejoiceth not in iniquity, but rejoiceth in the truth; beareth all things, believeth all things,hopeth all things, endureth all things. Charity never faileth: but whether there be prophecies, they shall fail; whether there be tongues, they shall cease; whether there be knowledge, it shall vanish away.

For we know in part, and we prophesy in part. But when that which is perfect is come, then that which is in part shall be done away. When I was a child, I spake as a child, I understood as a child, I thought as a child: but when I became a man, I put away childish things.

For now we see through a glass, darkly; but then face to face: now I know in part; but then shall I know even as also I am known. And now abideth faith, hope, charity, these three; but the greatest of these is charity.

(I Cor 13:1-13)

The other Apostles affirmed that this was the essential message of Jesus the Christ, and Paul was both humbled and surprised. His head knew that what he said came, in part, from Plato's Cave myth: *For now we see through a glass, darkly; but then face to face.* But his heart knew that the passage on charity arose from his own rebellious and loveless childhood. From that burning personal experience, his words trembled with truth.

During that second trip of many years, he wrote to the Christians in Rome. In that letter, he went stylistically far beyond anything he had written before. He re-created the experience of his conversion, speaking as if from a world far beyond the human:

> *O the depth of the riches both of the wisdom and knowledge of God! How unsearchable are his judgments, and his ways past finding out! For who hath known the mind of the Lord? Or who hath been his counselor? Or who hath first given to him, and it shall be recompensed unto him again?*
>
> *For of him, and through him, and to him, are all things: to whom be glory for ever. Amen.* (Romans 11:33-36)

Re-reading it, Paul muttered to himself, "I didn't write that!" The passage glowed with transcendence. Most people reading it called the style "ecstatic", and indeed, Paul had difficulty understanding where that strain of writing had come from. He saw himself as rational and phlegmatic. This sounded more like John than John did himself.

Paul remained troubled by his personal ability to transcend himself. His habitual mode of writing was pedestrian—much more as he saw himself. His years living on the seamy side of life had left him with few illusions. He knew first-hand the world of desires, and he knew how often the ascetic appearance—with money—concealed fleshly practices. Wherever he traveled, few could fool him. It was as if he knew all the workings of the human heart and appetites.

His insight and awareness colored his speaking and his letters. When he wrote back to places where he had proselytized—from the Corinthians on—they felt that he was there in person, as if he had known or anticipated each temptation that plucked away at the fabric of their new-found faith. His special interest and focus—almost the mark of his ministry—was his constant admonition and warning against the powers of the world that could distract a person from the world-beyond-death. He knew that these sections of his letters had two origins: from his experience as a thief and bandit, and from his early Greek schooling—from a Platonic myth in *Phaedrus*—the myth of the charioteer.

Plato pictured the soul driving a chariot pulled by two horses. One horse was white and long necked, well bred, well behaved, and ran upward toward the light without a whip. The other was black and short-necked, badly bred, troublesome. The white horse represented rational and moral impulses—the virtuous part of human nature, seeking knowledge of the good, the true, and the one. The black horse represented the irrational passions, and carnal appetites—the vicious part of human nature seeking satisfaction and contentment. The Charioteer's task was to control and direct the horses. How the charioteer drove the horses determined his choice for reason and virtue, or his choice for appetite and vice. Paul loved the myth, and sensed himself as the charioteer, reining in the black horsse and giving rein to the white one.

Through his first two journeys of ministry, he strove to give his white horse the lead on the chariot he was driving.

V

Years later, when he returned to Jerusalem after his third trip, he learned that his father had died. At the family home, he found his mother unchanged but old. Daniel had fulfilled all his youthful promise of smiling hypocrisy.

His mother looked at Paul in shock and shook her head, saying, "Your father read your letters and the last thing he said was 'What a great teacher Solomon would have been.' Then he died. You were always a disappointment to him."

Paul nodded, "I know, I know."

"But," Daniel cut in, "you always thought you were right."

Paul looked from one to the other. How could they understand him or his transcendent conversion? They had disowned him before he was 25! Only now, years later, did he feel the depth of the alienation. When he returned to the Apostles, his emotional emptiness was filled only by his faith.

Daniel denounced Paul secretly to the Roman commander in Jerusalem for seditious acts as a Christian and for provoking revolt against Rome. At the same time, he reminded that commander about Paul's career as Bar-Abbas, the notorious brigand. When arrested, Paul exercised his right as a Roman citizen to be tried by Roman law, and with no Roman governor in Judaea, he was shipped for trial to Rome.

The trip was interrupted by a shipwreck on the island of Malta, but Paul finally arrived at the centre of worldly power. He was condemned to death, and knew that nothing could save him.

From Solomon Bar-Levin through Sol Bar-Abbas and Saul of Cilicia to Paul of Tarsus—Paul had seen it all. In knowledge he had passed beyond all his instructors. He had journeyed with twists and turns from sin to saintliness. On that journey, Paul recognized the saving power of faith through his good works of preaching and example. His own experience filled him with hope for those to whom he preached, for none could have started as low as he himself had been, at the door of death as a criminal. And none could have experienced the saving power of the Prophet Jesus Christ as he had done both literally and figuratively.

In the days before execution, he accepted with greater and greater conviction the answer to his question, "Why was I sent back?" He could say with humility and truth what he had written to Timothy,

> *"I have fought the good fight of faith; I have tried to lay hold on eternal life whereunto I felt called; and I have professed a good profession before many witnesses." (1 Timothy: 6:12)*

THE END

NOTES

The following seven Epistles are viewed as authentic, the work of Paul of Tarsus. The dates of composition are those generally agreed on.

Date	Name
51	1st Thessalonians
52-54	Philippians
52-54	Philemon
53-54	1st Corinthians
55	Galatians
55-56	2nd Corinthians
55-58	Romans

The composition for the four Gospels present a greater range of years for their writing. Two of the ranges are printed below

Mark	55-70	68-73	60's (early)
Matthew	50-70	70-100	80's (early)
Luke	55-62	59-63	90's
John	80's	85-100	90's (late)

The ranges are great, but scholars generally agree that the Epistles of Paul preceded the Gospels. The interplay between Gospels and Epistles presents many problems. Since Paul never knew Jesus Christ, his knowledge rests on his claim of direct revelation, and word of mouth from disciples and apostles who knew him.

There are inconsistencies between the Jesus Christ of the Gospels and the Jesus Christ of the Pauline Epistles. It is impossible to judge whether or not the Gospels were written as a corrective to Paul's Epistles.

The Other Ring

INTRODUCTION TO THE OTHER RING

The basis of this story lies in the work of J.R.R. Tolkien. I was in my late twenties when I encountered The Lord of the Rings, and because volume one, The Fellowship of the Ring, was not in the library, I started with volume two, The Two Towers. At that time, I could start anywhere and read the beginning later. Within half a dozen pages I came to the lament for Boromir, and I realized that I was in the grasp of a master linguist and a great poet. Tolkien's world, with its long history—a history that placed mankind in Tolkien's fourth age—that world assumed a reality that challenged the world I lived in. I read, re-read, and re-re-read The Lord of the Rings, adding The Hobbit and The Silmarillion. The consistency in history, the varieties in language, and the many cultures left me in awe.

From that whole work, though, the Elven Rings fascinated me more than anything else.

Vilya, Elrond's sapphire Ring held in Imladris (Rivendell) was the Ring of air. Nenya, Galadriel's diamond Ring which was revealed to Frodo in Lothlorien was the Ring of water. Narya, Gandalf's ruby Ring, was the Ring of fire.

The One Ring and the other Rings—nine for men, seven for Dwarves, and one for Sauron himself—seemed somehow lesser. They were connected to power, but the three Elven Rings were elemental—connected to air, water, and fire.

For this story to make sense to readers, some historical background material will precede the story itself.

Historical Background

The First Age of Middle Earth ended when the Valar, the supernatural powers who had shaped Middle Earth (under the direction of Eru, the One), came out of the Far West and joined with Elves and Men at Thangorodrim to defeat Melkor. They bound him outside time forever. The Maia called Sauron hid himself and lived on unrepentant. Some of

Melkor's creatures—spirits of flame called Balrogs and other shadow creatures—survived in hidden places of the world.

The Second Age (1-3441) saw the rise and fall of Numenor and the forging of all the Rings: nine for men, seven for Dwarves, three for elves, and one for Sauron himself. That age ended with the last union of Elves and Men under Gil Galad when Sauron was vanquished and the One Ring was cut from his hand. But Sauron was not destroyed, and continued into the Third Age (1-3141) as a spirit, later growing a body and knowing that the One Ring, though lost, still existed.

The Third Age ended after the destruction of Sauron when the three Elven Rings sailed on the last ship crafted by Cirdan the Shipwright into the West (3021). For a time, however, some powers of the Third Age lingered on. The powers waned with the death of Aragorn in Gondor, and the passing of his wife, Arwen Undomiel, in the shadows of Lothlorien (3141). That same year, Legolas the Elf built a craft and with Gimli the Dwarf, they sailed into the West.

All the Rings forged in the Second Age passed after the Third Age. The One was destroyed when it fell into Orodruin, Mount Doom. The seven for Dwarves were lost—either to Sauron, or in the caves of the Dwarf-lords. And of the nine Rings for Mortal Men, eight were destroyed with the Nazgûl at Mount Doom.

> Bk VI Chapter 3 Mount Doom (5th last paragraph): *And into the heart of the storm . . . the Nazgûl came, shooting like flaming bolts, as caught in the fiery ruin of hill and sky, they crackled, withered and went out.*

There is no word of what happened to the Ring belonging to the Witch-king of Angmar, the Nazgûl destroyed by Éowyn on the Pelennor Fields:

> Bk V Chapter 6 Paragraph 21: *Then . . . she drove her sword between crown and mantle . . . but lo! the mantle and hauberk were empty.*

Since all of its power derived from the One Ring, that power was lost when the One was destroyed, and it could survive only as a metal hoop, impotent, dead.

The three Rings for the Elves survived the destruction of the One, but their power was diminished. Celebrimbor had forged them independently of Sauron, but with his instruction. From the time that he was aware of Sauron forging the One Ring, the Elves hid their Rings, or used them only at necessity.

> Silmarillion: Of the Rings of Power and the Third Age (283-304) (287) *Now the Elves made many rings . . . Narya, Nenya, and Vilya, the rings of Fire, Water, and Air—ruby, adamant and sapphire . . . . (298*

Each Ring had its own sphere of power. Vilya, the sapphire Ring of air was held by Elrond at Rivendell. He showed the elemental power of his Ring at the Ford of Bruinen:

> Book II Chapter 1 Many Meetings: *"Who made the flood?" asked Frodo. "Elrond commanded it," answered Gandalf. "the river of this valley is under his power and it will rise in anger when he has great need to bar the Ford."*

Nenya, the adamant Ring of Water, was held by Galadriel. In her mirror, formed when she poured water into a basin, Frodo could see things afar off. She gave Frodo a small phial filled with water from her mirror as a light for him in dark places. And Frodo saw the ring shine on her finger when he visited Lothlorien.

> Book II Chapter 7 The Mirror of Galadriel: *"Yes," she said . . . "it is not permitted to speak of it . . . . Verily it is in the land of Lórien upon the finger of Galadriel that one of the Three remains. This is Nenya, the Ring of Adamant . . . ."*

Narya, the ruby Ring of Fire was held first by Cirdan, the shipwright. When the Wizards came to Middle Earth, Cirdan recognized in Gandalf the one whose task was the destruction of Sauron, and gave him the Ring, saying, *"Something like this may be a warmth to you and others in dark places."* Gandalf called on all the powers of the Ring of Fire in Moria when he confronted the Balrog:

> Book II Chapter 5 The Bridge of Khazad-Dûm: *"You cannot pass," he said . . . "I am a servant of the Secret Fire, wielder of the Flame of Anor. The dark fire will not avail you, flame of Ûdun. Go back to the shadow. You cannot pass."*

Such were the three Rings that passed, we are told, into the Far West when the last ship sailed—the Rings of Air, of Water, and of Fire on the hands of Elrond, Galadriel, and Gandalf. And now we are ready for the story. As promised, it will start with "What if?"

Prologue

What if there had been a fourth Ring connected to the Elven Rings? If the elements air, water, and fire each empowered an Elven Ring, why not the element earth? What if there had been a fourth Ring—a Ring of Earth set with an emerald?

Here is the story of that other Ring of Power—the Ring of Earth. Its forging and its powers, along with its relationship to the other Elven Rings, will be dealt with in this story.

The Story

I

In 1550 (Second Age) the Elven-smiths in Eregion reached the height of their skill. Eregion lay conveniently just west of the gate to Khazad-dûm, Moria, the underground kingdom of the Dwarves. With instruction at first from Sauron, Celebrimbor the master-smith with the other Elven-smiths began forging the Rings of Power with the precious metals and gemstones provided by the Dwarves. Sauron specified nine rings of one kind for men, and seven rings of another kind for Dwarves. Celebrimbor turned those rings over to Sauron, but refused to make the three rings that Sauron specified for the Elves. He said that there were other artifacts he wished to make first, and then he himself would craft the Elven rings. Sauron accepted the sixteen rings and returned to Mordor.

Celebrimbor had already designed the three rings for the elves, but he mistrusted Sauron, and so concealed his plans.

Durin IV reigned in Moria when Celebrimbor was in Eregion. Between 1575 and 1590 in the Second Age, the friendship between Elves and Dwarves reached its highest point. In those years Celebrimbor began the three Elven rings, and he required mithril with three specific gemstones: a diamond, a sapphire, and a ruby. The Dwarves of course supplied the Elves with *mithril* and gemstones. Visits between Durin IV and Celebrimbor became common.

Tirella was the fourth and last child of Durin IV. She had three older brothers, and grew up in their shadow. She could have faded into obscurity like other Dwarf women, but she competed with her brothers and could smithy and forge as well as they did. Her taste went more to ornaments and jewels than it did to swords and axes, but her workmanship was superb.

Early she had asked Durin for her own forge high in Moria near an air vent. At her tiny forge and smithy, she learned the art of shaping and forming the metals from the earth. She might have confined herself to practical or even abstract shapes, but a vine poked its head through her air vent. Each day Tirella saw it grow into her smithy until, one day, it turned on itself, and throwing out tiny tendril ringlets, it grew back up on itself to the air vent and to the outer world.

Tirella watched the plant in awe. Its growth and movement amazed her, and the delicacy of the leaves, stems, and tendrils left her with a desire to create artifacts with vines as the inspiration. She walked out the eastern gate of Moria and climbed up the mountain to look at that vine by her air vent. She was struck by the persistent and steady growth of all vegetation. She saw in earth two conflicting powers. With the first power, the capacity to bind and hide metals, she was completely familiar. With the second power, the capacity to grow forth infinite varieties of trees, plants, and grasses, she had never considered. Her astonishment grew the more she examined them. Before, she had never paid attention to vegetation; now everything about it awed her.

Each vine was an individual, shaped by where it had started to grow, and by its environment. She could no longer think *vines.* They were a group of unique individual vines. She began to reproduce in metal and gemstones the shapes of leaves, and the relation of leaf to stem to root. At first it was difficult for her because vines grew and changed steadily in green curves, but with time and practice, she mastered the problem.

She created jewelry from the gemstones that came from the mines, but her inspiration for the jewelry came from vegetation. On her tiny wheel she shaped the metal and gemstones with dust of adamant into vines and flowers.

In those years, Tirella often accompanied her father to Eregion where the Elven smiths worked. A bond of affection grew between Celebrimbor and Tirella. He looked at some of the jewelry she made, and said half-jokingly that she was a craftsman in the line of Fëanor himself, that master-craftsman who had forged the silmarils in the Uttermost West. But in his heart, Celebrimbor knew that this was no joke. Tirella, young as she seemed, was his equal in the jeweler's art.

Both Dwarves and Elves felt that her association with the Elves modified her appearance. She was blond, pale, slender and delicate-looking, but like all of her race, she was strong and resilient.

Between 1585 and 1590, Celebrimbor forged the three Great Rings without any direction from the Lord of the Dark Tower. These were the years when Tirella accompanied her father on his visits to Celebrimbor, delivering sometimes mithril, sometimes gemstones. The three Rings required both mithril and time. Tirella and her father delivered the mithril, and often Tirella stayed to watch the great craftsman at work.

On one occasion, there was discussion and then debate between Durin, Celebrimbor, and Tirella.

"From the dead earth with my smelter I can purify metals and hold them in their pristine state. That is what I bring to you, Celebrimbor, to shape by your craft," Durin IV claimed.

"True," said Celebrimbor, "and in the fires of my smithy, I forge not only your iron, tin, lead, and other dead metals, but mithril itself into my creations."

Tirella shook her head, saying, "They are all alive. They don't breathe and breed, but they have a life and a life span. The radiant metals fade with age and transmute themselves to lesser metals. Except for gold and mithril, the metals you forge long to return to the earth. Just as iron rusts in its desire to join with earth again, your other metals bind with air to resume their life in the earth."

"That isn't life," her father said. "Those are long processes, and there is no exercise of will or choice in matters drawn from the earth."

"Not will or choice as we know it, Lord," Tirella responded, "but there is a growth toward the earth in knives and swords. It takes our resistance to stop their efforts to escape to the ground from which they came. A stone bridge may last as long as the earth itself, but an iron bridge is doomed to fall back to the earth from which it was separated."

From then she was silent. Durin and Celebrimbor argued on with no conclusion. Tirella knew that while fire could wrench apart the contents of earth, air and water slowly returned them to their native state.

And they did not consider, nor did she mention, the earth as the source of life. From its depths came not only ore and gemstones, not only metal and jewels, but also the wealth of vegetation from which all life grew.

During her visits, she observed the single-minded concentration with which Celebrimbor forged and cast the three Rings for the Elves. She watched him name the Rings with the runes of Fëanor: *Air, Water, Fire.* He had solved the difficult task of setting the gemstones in the molten mithril without destroying the stones. Back in Moria at her own forge, she set about casting a ring like the work of Celebrimbor in imitation of all vegetation with an emerald.

When she started to work the mithril, she saw flowers, leaves, and vines. And when she saw the emerald, she saw all vegetation and pondered as she worked about earth with its dual powers—to turn metals into ore with air and water, and to grow forth all vegetation with the same elements, water and air.

She worked slowly melting the mithril in fire and cooling it in water. The ring itself was a slender circle of mithril intertwined with vines which almost concealed the skeleton circle. She broadened it at the top and shaped four tiny pillars of mithhril that were to enclose the emerald. On those tiny pillars she elevated the runes of Fëanor that spelled *earth.* As she worked, she thought only of the earth which provided her with mithril, and of the earth which grew the living vegetation. She sensed that she was joining those two powers of the earth with mithril and emerald, ore and vegetation, into this ring.

There was a technical problem. She had to heat the mithril until it was ductile, set the emerald in place, force down the four mithril clasps, and plunge the ring into water before the molten metal could destroy the emerald. Three times she had reached this point. Once the emerald was misshapen by the heat; one time the emerald slipped out as she twisted the fourth clasp, and once the clasps were not hot enough to bend. This fourth time, everything worked, and it seemed to her that the earth trembled when the ring was plunged into cold water. Her emerald was more brittle than any of the stones Celebrimbor had used, and so her success was a miracle in the jeweler's art.

All unknowingly she had forged a Ring of Power, single-mindedly focusing not just on the task, but on the element whose power the Ring absorbed through her intense concentration, through the vegetation and landscape she etched in the setting around the stone, and then through naming that element with runes.

As the mithril setting locked the stone into place, Celebrimbor was aware of a power in Moria, and Sauron, in his Dark Tower, felt a force coming from the direction of Eregion, but neither could sense either the person or the nature of the power. Tirella didn't speak of her ring to her father Durin IV, but with a shy sense of pride she showed it to Celebrimbor.

"What beautiful work you have done!" he said, gazing at the ring of mithril with the gleaming green emerald. As he took the ring, he said, "I believe that I would have shattered the emerald . . ." He fell silent. He remained silent as he gazed into the green depths of the stone, saw the tiny moss and leaves in mithril around the emerald, and looked at the runes raised cameo-style. He continued silent as he handed the ring back to Tirella.

"Tell me, how did you raise the runes for *earth* in the mithril?"

"I lifted away tiny fragments of mithril as I heated and re-heated it, while I shaped the receptacle for the emerald-stone."

He touched her arm gently. "I could not have done that," he murmured. "You are an amazing craftsman—or craftswoman," he laughed, then was silent. "It's a Ring of Power!" he said after a moment. "Did you know that?"

Tirella shook her head. "No. I simply tried to focus on the work like you. What do you mean? What power?" Tirella asked. "I feel something when I put it on," she said, "but I know nothing about power."

"It has powers connected with the runes you raised—with *earth*—but hide it until you learn and master its powers," he advised. "Come more often to see me!"

Tirella was pleased and happy with praise from such a smith, and concealed the Ring from everyone as he had advised.

The first power she experienced was an increased perception. She could sense the composition of earth and rock, and like a water-dowser, she could find seams of the best ore. All she had to do was wear the Ring and hold some of the desired metal or gemstone in her hand. What other powers would it confer? And how could she discover those powers?

She designed and executed the West Gate of Moria, working mithril into the stones beside and above the gate. She inscribed in Elven script the charm that would work the door, "Say Friend And Enter." The runes were almost invisible by day, because the mithril writing was so fine. But in moonlight, they shone with an otherworldly fire.

She had scarcely finished the work at the door when, in 1600, Sauron forged the One Ring at his smithy in the Chamber of Fire in Orodruin. Celebrimbor summoned Tirella, and she hurried to him.

He drew her aside and said, "Beware now! The Dark Lord has forged a Master Ring to control all the others. Take care when you use your Ring because even though you took no instruction from him, you imitated me, someone who took his personal instruction in the forging of Rings for his purposes."

"Can I use it at all?" Tirella asked, "or will he master me?"

"I can't say now," Celebrimbor answered. "But though you wear it all the time, use its powers for only brief hours."

"Are any others in danger?" she asked.

"There are seven Dwarves involved. In my heart I heard the Dark Lord, as he completed his Ring, talk of three Rings for the Elves, seven Rings for the Dwarves, nine Rings for mortal Men, and one Ring for himself:

One ring to rule them all; One ring to find them
One ring to bring them all; and in the darkness bind them.

He doesn't know of your Ring, and so for now you're safe. Use its powers, as I said, as seldom as possible."

Tirella left with fear in her heart, but stalwart and sturdy of purpose, like all her race, she determined to test the powers in her Ring.

When she touched plants, they thrived. When she gestured, plants moved. She could drive trees into a frenzy of branch-waving when there was no wind. And finally, when she talked to any vegetation from moss through vegetables and fruit to bushes, vines, and trees, they seemed to pause and listen, even in a wind.

But all of these things happened only when she was wearing the Ring.

Fellow Dwarves stared at her because often she talked to vegetation unaware of any audience around her. They looked sideways at her, and no proposals of union came to her father.

Her brothers looked concerned. She would have to leave them every couple of centuries because she didn't change or age. She would have to re-invent herself.

In 1640, with her father's permission, she passed through Eregion and went westward toward what became known as the Pass of Rohan. There she met the Ents of Fangorn Forest. They had a power and affinity with the whole green world of vegetation that Tirella loved. Their language was like the forests and trees themselves, many-layered, full of the history of whatever was the subject, and ancient beyond telling.

Their forests were full of great oak and hardwood trees with conifers, but she saw no fruit trees like apple and peach, and no flowering bushes, vines, or creepers. When Tirella asked Fangorn why bushes and fruit trees weren't there, he explained, "The Entwives took them when they moved east. They prefer gardens and orchards like those grown by men to the forests that we guard and keep. So they moved east to where men live."

"So will there be no Entings?" she asked.

"Not for the present," they said, "but the Entwives will return soon."

"What reason will they have for returning?" she asked. Fangorn and the other Ents hummed and sang in their incomprehensible language, but gave no reply to her question.

The Ents had a power that lay outside anything Tirella had seen. She lingered on there for many years, searching through the layers of green growth with the life and power of the trees themselves. She marveled at the complexity of Ent speech, and at the vastness of their memories of things and times past. The Ents in turn marveled at her ability to communicate with vegetation, but they were not curious about how she had that power.

She was still with them in 1693 when the war of the Elves and Sauron began. When the Ents told her of it—information they gathered from birds—Tirella sped east through Eriador and into Moria just before 1695, when Sauron's forces invaded the lands west of the mountains. Eregion was laid waste, and Celebrimbor was destroyed. Orcs from Sauron's army invaded and infested the west halls and chambers of Moria before the Dwarves could close the gate.

Tirella grieved for the loss of her mentor Celebrimbor, but with the grief came an anger that energized her. With her ring, Tirella could hurl rocks, raise dust, and cause local tremors in the earth. The orcs fled before those attacks, seemingly from the ground itself. They scurried through the western gate where a lake of fetid water had gathered. Sauron had planted a twelve-armed kraken in the lake to guard the gate. As the orcs fled, the kraken seized them for food. The Dwarves, having watched the fate of the orcs, closed the western gate.

In the safety of their underground kingdom, the Dwarves heard how Sauron and his army swept down along the great river driving all his foes to the coast. There they met a huge fleet from Numenor under King Tar-Minastir who landed an army that routed Sauron and his forces, driving them back over the mountains to Mordor. There he brooded in rage, plotting revenge.

The Westlands had peace. There were few changes in Moria, except that there was almost no demand for metal and gemstones.

II

How to manage her agelessness? The only solution she could see was to leave the Dwarves every couple of centuries to return as a younger version of herself. Just as her father was in a line of Durins who had been called deathless resembling each other so much, she knew that she would have to become Tirella II, and Tirella III, and so on with perhaps other names. Without consulting her father, she began a trip eastward to reinvent herself.

At the same time as Tirella left Moria for her journey east, Sauron began moving eastward from Mordor to enlist the support and help of men, easily seduced by his promise of power and wealth.

Tirella passed ahead of him, unaware of his movements behind her. She traveled far into the east, quietly and alone. She was fearless, having mastered the powers of her Ring over earth and vegetation. Vines whipped up at her thought, clouds of dust rose from dry land, and clods of earth flew where she directed.

As she moved south toward pleasanter weather, she noticed furrows and trails she could not recognize. The farther she went, the clearer the trail appeared. The she saw them—a moving grove.

Stealthily, as Dwarves can move, she crept nearer and heard them talking. She recognized the Entwives.

"What are you doing so far from your homes?" she called out in Elvish.

The Entwives stopped, and two of the taller ones called out in the Common Speech, "Who are you? An Elf? And aren't you far from your own home?"

Tirella spoke now in the Comon Speech, 'I'm Tirella, a Dwarf, daughter of During IV of Moria. You lived many days journey west of us. What are you doing this far east, and where are the Ents?"

The ones who had spoken tramped up to her. "I am Alder, and this is Lilac. We have left the Ents with their trees and forests. We wanted gardens, and fields with hedges. They wouldn't listen. We have already left behind Erica and Ling—Broom and Heather—you might have passed heaths.

"I didn't notice," Tirella said, "but where are you going?"

"We'll travel east to where men garden and we'll settle there."

"But what of the Ents? and—and what of Entings?"

"We're sure to find different races of Ents east of here—where there are large forests, there will be Ents! Our love is of gardens, of crops and fields, of hedge rows and copses. Our smaller friends, Ivy and Wisteria, look for walls."

"I'll travel with you?" Tirella said, and moved east with them.

They came to desert people who tried to break them up. Tirella raised first dust, and then a sandstorm that sent the men scampering back to their tents. The column of Entwives moved on.

In the foothills of giant mountains, Rhododendron left them, and the farther east they moved, the smaller their numbers became as the smaller trees and bushes found favorable ground.

Tirella saw changes in the humans they encountered. Dark brown darkened to black, and lightened again to brown, to red-brown, and finally to yellow.

In the mountains, they encountered men who attacked them. Tirella raised clods of earth that pelted them, and later she shook the earth in a quake. The attackers fled.

The last Entwife to leave was Mulberry. She settled among the yellow people who spun worm-thread into silk.

"This is my home!" she explained to Tirella. "I'll manage the small trees whose leaves feed the silkworms."

Alone again, Tirella returned to the west. She had learned to be invisible against any ground, and enjoyed her own company. "I'll return to the Dwarves as my own granddaughter," she planned to herself, and returned the way she had come. But how changed the terrain! Gardens and hedges of low-lying fences, the work of the Entwives, now clothed the landscape.

She met Dwarves from the Iron Hills, and presented herself as Tirella's grand-daughter. With them, she resumed her mining work.

In 1900 she worked in the Iron Hills with the Dwarves, but longed for the mines of Moria and her own special forge. She set off south from the Iron Hills, following the great river and reached Ithilien with its waterfalls and caves. She dwelt there restlessly for a time, but passed on to Khazad-dûm, Moria, again presenting herself as a descendant of herself.

The centuries of the second age unfolded. Tirella left Moria in 2100 to re-invent herself once more. In 2251 the Ringwraiths showed themselves for the first time. Tirella was in Mirkwood when they appeared and she felt their menace. The nine of them formed a force that she felt safest by avoiding. She returned once more to Moria, the kingdom under the mountain, and worked at her forge.

Over the next age she wandered the earth. In 2400, she traveled to the Old Forest south of Bree and met Tom Bombadil. Like her, he was devoted to the life of growing things, and exercised his power through enchantment in doggerel verse. He promoted growth and well-being in all vegetation, but particularly in the vegetation growing in water. This was the first person she had met with gifts and powers like her own. She admired the lushness of his river plants—lilies, reeds, and rich marshlands. and pointed to them as she spoke.

"What is that green ring I see on your hand?" he asked.

No one had asked her that question before, but Tirella knew that in this space which he had reserved for himself, there were no boundaries for him. Sensing his innocence, she replied "A ring I made imitating Celebrimbor, the Elven smith."

"That was centuries ago," Tom said, "and you're here. How can that be?"

"It's is a power of the Ring, to confer long life. Celebrimbor told me that it was a Ring of Power endowed with the power of the earth itself."

"I heard that he was instructed by the Dark Lord to make other Rings for Men, for the Dwarves, and for Elves. And I learned that he was instructed to make three Rings for the Elves—of *Air*, of *Water*, and of *Fire*."

"Yes," she replied, "and Celebrimbor forged all of those Rings before his instructor forged the One Ring to control all the others."

"Let me see it!" Tom exclaimed.

Without hesitation she handed it to him. He looked at it closely, and flipped it into the air. Flashes of silver and green spurted from it like a tiny day-star. He caught it, and handed it back.

"Why didn't the Dark Lord instruct Celebrimbor to forge that element—*earth*—when he specified the three other elements, *air*, *water*, and *fire*?"

"I don't know," Tirella replied slowly, surprised by the question.

Tom's attention moved from the Ring to his vegetation, and they did not speak of it again.

But the question remained in Tirella's heart when she wandered on.

She observed and respected the limits Tom Bombadil had set for himself, but she would never confine her movements as he had done.

From the Old Forest, she traveled northeast through what became Mirkwood where she was almost destroyed by Trolls. Their power over stone forced her to retreat before them. Light was their weakness, and she knew their power derived from some unknown darkness.

With the Beornings around 2700 she found herself with primitive man-animals who were shape-changers. Their power again was something new to her, and they remained a mystery though she admired their devotion to animals and plants.

She returned to Moria, and settled there to work once more at her forge. But even in the deep changeless caverns of Khazad-dûm she and all the Dwarves sensed the passage of Sauron with his armies of easterlings and orcs westward once again. Sauron drove all the forces and powers of the west before him to the shore of the ocean at Umbar.

But there at Umbar, once more, he was defeated. Ar-Pharazon, 24th King of Numenor, landed and the splendour of his fleet was such that Sauron's forces deserted him to join the magnificence of Numenor's power. Sauron abased himself and was taken, a willing prisoner, to Numenor.

Tirella worked in her smithy at Moria again as a descendant of herself through the half-century in which Sauron seduced the powers of Numenor, and convinced Ar-Pharazon that he had the right to claim the Ultimate West.

In 3319, when Ar-Pharazon sailed west, breaking the Ban of the Valar, Numenor sank beneath the waves, Ar-Pharazon and his fleet were destroyed, and Sauron returned to earth as a malevolent spirit with no body. He could never again assume an appearance that was pleasant, and he brooded in Mordor once more over his repeated defeats by the powers of elves and men.

After a century, Sauron, assuming the name of the Lidless Eye, attacked Gondor in 3429, and took Minas Ithil. A year later, the Last Alliance of Elves and Men marched against Sauron and drove him back to Barad-dur. The siege lasted 7 years. Finally Sauron came out himself to fight his enemies. Barad-dur was overthrown, Sauron was defeated, and the One Ring was cut from his finger. Isildur, claiming the Ring, refused to destroy it. Sauron became a spirit without shape, and the Ringwraiths disappeared. So ended the second age.

III

When the One Ring was cut from Sauron's finger, Tirella, working in Moria, felt her whole being wrenched in a spasm. A few years later, when Isildur lost the One Ring in the river Anduin at the Gladden Fields, Tirella fell into a coma. She was put to bed by the Dwarves. When she stayed asleep and didn't die, they carved a bed for her, and built a vault of crystal over the bed frame. Her fame grew in Dwarf circles, but the rest of the world knew nothing of the deathless sleeping Dwarf princess. When they traveled from Moria, they carried Tirella with them, and so the first centuries of the Third Age unfolded.

After 1300 years, evil things began to multiply. Orcs increased in the Misty Mountains, and began to attack the Dwarves. The Nazgûl reappeared. And Tirella awakened in the Iron Hills.

When she listened to the story of her sleep for the previous millennium, she knew that Sauron was taking shape again, and that the One Ring had not been destroyed. As Celebrimbor had suspected, her ring was bound to both Sauron and his One Ring in some way, but he had said that her Ring of Earth was not wholly subject to his One Ring. But then, she asked herself, why had she fallen asleep?

In 1100 the Istari, the wizards, came out of the west. She intuited that they had come to battle with Sauron, and she set out to meet them.

On her way west she was apprehended in Lothlorien and brought before Celeborn and Galadriel. She explained herself at first as a descendant of the Dwarf princess who had slept through a thousand years, but she felt an awe for the innate majesty, power, and wisdom of the two Elves, and decided, on an impulse, to reveal her Ring to them.

"I was indirect with you before. I am that Dwarf princess who slept the thousand years. When Celebrimbor was forging the three rings for the Elves, I forged this Ring in imitation of him and of his work, and I showed it to him."

Galadriel took the ring and raised it to her eyes, but stopped. "It's a Ring of Power. And it has given you ageless life. What did he say when he saw it?"

"Like you, he said it was a Ring of Power, and I had forged it with all my concentration on the element it embodied—*earth.* He thought it was not subject to the One Ring of the Dark Lord."

"Oh! He was wrong! It is not in his consciousness as are all the other Rings, but you imitated Celebrimbor for the forging. That was why, when the One Ring slipped from Isildur's finger in the river Anduin, you fell asleep."

"Why did I sleep?" Tirella asked. "I don't understand."

"When the Ring left the hand of Isildur, it lost its own attachment to earth—that is, no longer on his hand. Your Ring cast you into sleep because though your ring is not dominated by the One, its attachment to earth as element is connected to the One. And in the Anduin river, your ring was suspended in another element—water—and lost its attachment to earth. So the two of you—Ring and bearer—slept until the owner of the One Ring awoke."

"When I woke up, did that mean that the One Ring was found?"

"I don't think so. You woke because Sauron, by re-forming himself, knew that his Ring had not been destroyed. He is looking for it now, and so you are awake."

"When the Dark Lord instructed Celebrimbor in the forging of the three Elven Rings, of water, fire, and air, why didn't he instruct him for the fourth element—*earth*?" There, she thought to herself, I have asked Tom Bombadil's question.

Galadriel turned from Tirella to Celeborn, and they both looked at her. "Let me see the Ring." Celeborn asked. Tirella handed it to him.

He looked into its depths, weighed it in his and, and returned it to her, all in a silence that hung in the air.

"I don't know, and I've never considered that question. But perhaps his One Ring, of gold alone, derives its power from a part of the element *earth*, because he looked only for power. Your Ring, by contrast, takes its inspiration from the whole element—*earth*—that binds ore and grows vegetation, and though connected to his Ring, is somehow separate from his One Ring."

"Or greater than . . ." Galadriel added.

Tirella nodded her head at Celeborn's explanation, but frowned and shook her head at Galadriel's addition. Galadriel reached forward and took her hand.

"You are right," she said. "His Ring is greater, for he himself is greater than any of us. But your vision of the two properties of earth endows your Ring with broader power than his and," she went on looking at Celeborn, "limits his vision of his own element. The power of your Ring may survive the destruction of his."

"But I slept for one thousand years," Tirella said.

Celeborn said, "We'll never know, but his limited vision of his own element—earth—may work against him and hasten his destruction."

"So use it as you will," Galadriel advised.

"I'm going to seek the five Wizards. Should I tell them about my Ring?"

"No. Like Elrond and myself, guard it closely, and use it only at necessity," Galadriel advised.

Tirella felt relieved to have shared her Ring with the Lord and Lady of Lothlorien. She was ready to move on.

When she left Lothlorien, she passed through Moria to the western gate. She hurried past the lake of the kraken, and passed swiftly through the new kingdoms of Arnor and Gondor, founded by the followers of Gil-Galad, who had escaped with some of the faithful from Numenor when it was sunk into the sea.

She failed to meet all five of the wizards, but she met three. Saruman in his greeting dismissed her. She felt his lack of interest. Radagast was a kindred spirit interested in animals and vegetable forms of life. Gandalf was interested in her as a Dwarf, and he asked her to take him to Moria. She guided him through the western gate and the passages to the throne room of Durin VI, the King of the Dwarves in the Third Age. Gandalf continued with her through the rest of the underground kingdom of the Dwarves, and they made their goodbyes at the eastern gate. He wished to go first to Lothlorien, and then to the Dunedain in the north. She wanted to work at her forge.

When the plague came in 1636, the Dwarves were safe in Moria out of all contact with earth, but once more the market for precious metals fell off as men, Elves, Dwarves and orcs died on earth-surface. At her forge, she sketched the pattern of a small mithril body coat for herself but did not feel driven to start it.

After the plague, the desire for jewels and the market for metals grew. Over three centuries, for the stated purpose of finding gems and metal, Tirella led the Dwarves through the mines of Moria.

She left briefly after a century to renew herself. On her return, finding a vein of mithril, she led them deeper and deeper into Moria. But she led them too far. In 1980 they broke through into a fire pit and released a Balrog, a spirit of flame, living on from the First Age at the root of the mountains. The Balrog killed Durin VI and Náin his son. The Dwarves fled, leaving Moria to the Balrog, and to an infestation of orcs who worshipped that spirit of fire.

With the Dwarves, Tirella traveled to the Grey Hills, carrying with her all the mithril she had mined. She felt such guilt for having allowed her greed to release the Balrog that she was paralyzed. She could no longer assist the Dwarves, and retreated into a workshop assigned to her. There, slowly, she completed the small mithril coat for herself.

When Thráin in 1999 went to Erebor, the Lonely Mountain, Tirella accompanied him and through her Ring found the huge crystal which she shaped into the Arkenstone of Thráin, a light in the darkness of the caves. She shaped miracles of jewelry for Dale, for Rivendell, for the Dunedain in the north and for Thráin in his kingdom under the mountain. The hallmark of her products was the wealth of leaves and vegetation that ornamented her metalwork.

Tirella traveled once more to re-invent herself and to return as the grand-daughter of the sleeping Dwarf-Princess. Her bed with the crystal case had become a Dwarf treasure, and she found herself immortalized for her deathless sleep of one thousand years.

When Déagol found the One Ring in 2463, Tirella felt a pulse of power and knew that the Ring was abroad. She sensed its power in the Misty Mountains from 2470 when Sméagol hid himself in the caves there.

Three centuries later, in 2770, Smaug the dragon invaded the mountain with fire. He drove the Dwarves from their kingdom and burned Dale. Tirella fled, leaving her forge and the mithril cloak she had fashioned for herself. She went northeast with the Dwarves to the Iron Hills where she worked at finding metals for weapons that the Dwarves could shape in their forges to fight the dragon.

A century later she was still in the Iron Hills. When Thror set out to claim Moria, Tirella warned him of the Balrog, and explained how there was no power to control or destroy it. He queried her closely. How did she know of the Balrog? She told him that the story of the Balrog had passed mother-to-daughter since the desertion of Moria by the Dwarves in 1980.

As she had feared, Thror was slain but not by the Balrog. He was defeated and beheaded by the orc Azog. When Tirella heard of his death, she warned Dáin Ironfoot about the spirit of fire in Moria. She remained in the Iron Hills through the war between the Dwarves and the Orcs from 2793 to 2799. When Dáin slew Azog, he saw the Balrog, through the open door of Moria, and told the Dwarves why they had to abandon all plans of repossessing the mines of Khazad-dûm.

After Smaug the dragon had been slain, and after the Battle of the Five Armies in 2941, the Dwarves took over the lonely mountain once again. When Tirella looked for her mithril coat, she learned that Thorin Oakenshield had found it in the pile of treasure under Smaug, and had made a gift of it to Bilbo for his help in defeating the dragon. She said nothing, and that mithril coat passed in time from Bilbo to Frodo.

When Balin in 2989 wished to return to Moria, she warned him of the danger with the Balrog without confessing her own part in raising the spirit. He thanked her for the information, but with a band of Dwarves he moved back to Moria. No news returned, and Tirella hoped that all was well. But when he did not send back for more Dwarves to join him, she feared he had died.

The people in the north were unaware of the Council of Elrond and the formation of the Fellowship of the Ring. It took days and weeks for news of events unfolding in the south to reach the Lonely Mountain. The siege of Gondor, the death of the King of the Ringwraiths, and the initial defeat of Sauron's army with the raising of the siege of Gondor were happenings unknown in the north. What the Lonely Mountain and Dale experienced was an invasion of Sauron'e orcs and easterling in numbers that could have defeated them.

The fighting was worst through the spring of 3019, exactly at the time when Frodo was making his way through Mordor to Orodruin, the fiery mountain.

All the Dwarves and the living inhabitants of Dale had retreated to a last stand in the Lonely Mountain to fight against the orcs and the armies from the east. But on March 25, 3019, Tirella felt the release of her Ring, and sensed that the One Ring had been destroyed. Immediately the attacks from the orcs and Sauron's eastern armies at the Lonely Mountain dissolved. His power through the One Ring and his very existence were gone forever.

IV

Tirella traveled west and entered Moria with a vanguard of the Dwarves in September of 3019, after Aragorn had been crowned king. The cleansing of Khazad-Dûm was a long labour for the Dwarves. The upper halls with air vents took months to make habitable.

Two years later, working downward in the purification of their kingdom, Tirella sensed evil in the deeper tunnels where the Balrog had escaped from its prison. She sent the Dwarves back and advanced alone down the perilous passage. Shadow creatures and shadow shapes with glamours of evil rustled beyond her torch. With her ring, she drove a shield of rock before her, enclosing the shadows in the pit at the mountain's root were the Balrog had hidden itself. She called to the Dwarves for fire, and they threw burning torches into the dungeon, destroying the shadow creatures with light. She then sealed it off with a thick wall of rock.

In the depths of Moria, as she exercised the power of her Ring, she saw dimly, afar off, the Grey Havens and the gathering of the three Elven Rings on Elrond, Galadriel, and Gandalf to sail into the Undying Lands in the west. She reached out to them, and heard a talking vision.

The Elven Ringbearers of Middle Earth, with Bilbo and Frodo, were gazing back at the land that had been their home for so long. As it sank from sight, they all looked west toward their future, except Galadriel, who stared restlessly backward.

"What troubles you?" Celeborn asked.

"I can't say. I sense some power there that I don't understand," she said waving vaguely backward at Middle Earth.

"I felt it too," said Elrond. glancing at his ring Vilya, and clenching his fist.

"I feel nothing," Gandalf murmured. "Could the rings still have some power to sense evil, or could the Silmarils affect the rings?"

"We'll never know," Celeborn said. "Jewels from the first age and jewels from the second age—the high craft of Feänor and of Celebrimbor—who can say if they're linked?"

"There is another Ring," Galadriel began hesitantly. Then she and Celeborn told the other Ring-bearers of Tirella and the Ring of earth.

"Perhaps that is what you sensed," Gandalf said, "But even so I'll repeat my words at the last debate under the walls of Minas Tirith," Gandalf said. "Other evils there are that may come; for Sauron himself is but a servant or emissary. Yet it is not our part to master all the evils of the world, but to do what is in us for the succour of those years wherein we are set, uprooting the evil in the fields that we know so that those who live after may have clean earth to till. What weather they will have is not ours to rule."

Celeborn added, "With the passing of Sauron and the Third Age, the evils from the First and Second Ages pass. Now is the Fourth Age, the Age of Men. Our toils are past."

"Maybe," Galadriel murmured, "but even so my heart feels a power from our Age lingering in Middle Earth. Maybe it is Tirella's Ring. But it is only an unrest, not a warning. Perhaps it will pass."

"Let's leave our unrest," Cirdan said. "For better or worse Middle Earth is behind us, and we have yet to work out our place and relationship with the Powers in the Far West. Let us turn our thought to that."

Their debate continued as the sound of breakers faded behind them, and only the whisper of the winds and the wash of waters against the gray ship sighed in their ears.

Tirella's vision of them faded too where she stood in the mines of Moria. She knew that they had sensed her Ring.

With all evil creatures and their works destroyed, Tirella traveled with a troop of workers to the west gate which they reopened. Under her guidance they drained the lake. The kraken had died of starvation after all living creatures had abandoned the area.

Traveling west after the purging of Moria, Tirella made for Aglarond in Helm's Deep, the wonder of whose caves she had heard about in Moria. There she found Gimli and Legolas together. When she stood before them, they glanced at her and then turned to face her.

"You're a Dwarf woman," Gimli said. "Where were you . . ."

"That's a Ring of Power," Legolas interrupted. "How did you get it?"

"You're Gimli," Tirella started, "and yes, I'm a Dwarf woman. I'm the Dwarf princess who slept one thousand years." Then looking at Legolas, she went on, "I'm Tirella, the daughter of Durin IV from the second age. I made this Ring—this Ring of Power—in imitation of Celebrimbor. It's the Ring of earth."

Legolas extended his hand and she handed the Ring to him. Gimli leaned over and looked at it too.

"The other Rings of Power have been destroyed or gone into the West. Why is yours here?" Legolas asked.

"When I fashioned it, Celebrimbor told me it was not completely under the power of the One Ring because I took no instruction from the Dark Lord. He felt that it was connected in some way since I had imitated him, and his instruction came directly from the Dark Lord. Celeborn and Galadriel told me that the Dark Lord had assigned the three elements—air, water, and fire—to the Elves but had kept the element earth to himself. Celeborn thought that he had ignored the power of the earth to grow all life, and focused on power and gold. He thought that mine evoked both the power of the earth to bind metal and ore, and the power of the earth to bring forth the plants and vegetation necessary for life. But they weren't sure. You were members of the Fellowship. What do you think?"

Gimli responded at once, "The Lord and Lady of Lothlorien were right. Remember, Legolas, what Gandalf said at the Couincil of Elrond about the One Ring and the Dark Lord.

> *'For he is very wise and weighs all things to a nicety in the scales of his malice. But the only measure that he knows is desire, desire for power, and so he judges all hearts.'*

I understand now what Gandalf meant. The One Ring evoked only one power of earth—lust for gold and for power. Your Ring evoked all the powers of earth: the power to hide and hold ore and the power to bring forth plant life."

"So your Ring probably retains all its power. What do you plan to do?" Legolas asked.

"I haven't decided," Tirella replied. "But since you were members of the Fellowship, would you tell me the whole story of the One Ring's destruction."

Between them, Legolas and Gimli provided the story for Tirella, and when it was over, Legolas said, "Come with us into the West. I know how to construct the craft, and Gimli is coming with me."

"Do you think that the Powers in the West will accept two Dwarves?" Tirella asked. They laughed at this question but laid plans to meet at Erebor, the Lonely Mountain. They all three had many farewells to make before they departed.

Gimli and Legolas wanted to visit Edoras and Gondor together. Then they would part. Gimli wanted to spend time in Khazad-dûm—Moria—probably a good long time. Then he wanted to visit the Iron Hills and the Grey Hills before going to Erebor for a final visit with Dáin, still king under the mountain. Legolas wanted to visit Ithilien, and Loth Lorien where some Elven magic still lasted. Then he wanted to spend a long time in Mirkwood, his old home, before passing on to Erebor. There at the Lonely Mountain they could meet and depart together.

In her own final farewell trip, Tirella spent a long time at Gondor with Aragorn and Arwen. She told them of her Ring, about its making, and about its powers and use. They suggested that she should travel with Gimli and Legolas into the West. Arwen assured her, "Forged in imitation of

Celebrimbor and back to Fëanor, your Ring of power is your passport into the Uttermost West."

"That is what I plan," she confessed, "But I have many goodbyes to make before I leave."

Arwen took her hand. "Don't miss the last boat with Legolas. He is the only mariner left who knows the way."

From there she passed north to the Ents in Fangorn to give them news of the Entwives and of their labors in farms and fields near the dwellings of men.

"Will they return?" Fangorn asked.

Before responding, Tirella looked around at the antiquity and depths of these western forests, draped in vines and moss, with many of the Ents now almost always dreaming and drowsing. She turned to Fangorn, and said, "No. They have no reason to return to you. And you knew this when they left. This is no home for Entwives and Entings. This is your own graveyard. The Age of Men has come, and everything on earth will change. You can smell it in the air, and taste it in the water. Nothing will remain the same now."

"Will you stay here, or perhaps in Lothlorien?"

"No. I have made up my mind. I'll sail into the West."

"How can you do that?" Fangorn asked. "The way is closed."

"There is one elf left to pass west, and I'll travel with him."

"May your travels be blessed," Fangorn said, adding, "I still hope for the Entwives and their return."

"It is good to hope," Tirella replied, "But I fear the wait will be long. Farewell. May your trees live long and may your groves spread."

After they had parted, she moved eastward once more to Tom Bombadil's haven from the world to bid him goodbye, and thence to Erebor and the kingdom under the mountain. There she met Legolas and Gimli, both making their farewells, and prepared to pass with them into the Uttermost West.

So when Gimli and Legolas, the last of the Fellowship, sailed in 3141, Tirella sailed with them and was revealed at last to Gandalf, to Galadriel, and to Elrond. The four Rings of the four elements were together.

The three Ring-bearers gazed long at her, recognizing in her Ring the source of unease that Galadriel had felt when she sailed from the Grey Havens.

EPILOGUE

What happened back in Middle Earth after Tirella had sailed with the last Ring into the west?

When the Firstborn, the Elves, passed into the West, the vibrancy of their presence left the earth. Dawn and dark seemed, somehow, less radiant, and the days were duller, the nights darker, and the folk of Middle Earth who had known the Elves, grieved for their passing.

The orcs died off with the fall of their creator; Ents faded into remote woods and forests; Hobbits retreated into the shire where they dwelt in isolation and became creatures of folk-tale. The race of men, with no one to master them, now multiplied. For a time the Dunedain held the northern lands with Elven art and culture. The people from the east and south set up kingdoms in emulation of them. The Third Age lingered until the death of Aragorn. Then as the

Dunedain faded and died, the Fourth Age saw the rise of men to dominate the earth.

What of the Dwarves? What of the earthdwellers? Part of their fate was linked to the Seven Rings they had been given, but they had always possessed a native strength against total subjection to those rings. The Rings were destroyed, but the Dwarves lived on. They persisted in the tales of men, not as the proud masters in Moria, or as Kings under the Mountains in the north. They became quaint characters of fairy tales. Gone forever was their prestige of race. They disappeared, but they didn't die.

With Tirella, they might have forged kingdoms for themselves under mountains, but their power had passed with her Ring.

THE END